I0700669

WAR IS HELL.

A Tale of War and One Man's Search for Meaning

ARTHUR A. EDWARDS

War Is Hell: A Tale of War And One Man's Search for Meaning
Copyright © [2025] by **Arthur A. Edwards**

For permissions requests, contact:
Writersway Solutions, LLC
10685 Hazelhurst Dr STE B #38295
Houston, Texas, 77043, USA
www.writerswaysolutions.com
1-888-666-4258

The individuals shown in Shutterstock's stock imagery are models, and these images are used for illustrative purposes.

ISBN (Paperback): 978-1-962733-63-2
ISBN (Ebook): 978-1-962733-62-5

Printed in the United States of America

DEDICATION

To my daughter, Diana Marie Edwards

ONE

Memories fade as we grow older, but I'll never forget the last battles in World War II and our fight to liberate Burma from the enemy. It was a bloody time. No quarter was asked nor any given. The battle for Myitkyina was the worst I had ever seen, and I had been in many. If I lean back against this rock and close my eyes, I will tell it as the memories return. How do you describe a bloody hell?

Japanese troops were accurately lobbing mortar shells and firing machine guns at us. The bullets were landing around our men like hail making a continuous storm of unrelenting noise. Hot metal fragments whirled around our heads. I could see my friend, and our commander, Major Phil Jenkins trying to dig his body deeper into the ground but having no luck. He finally lifted his head to see if his regiment was surviving. I yelled at him to keep down. It wasn't pretty. The smell of death was the all around us.

Through the smoke and dust the major could just make out his men trying to hide in the Burmese soil, in hopes that the shells and bullets would not find them. We all watched as men were blown to bits by incoming mortar and machine gun rounds.

"Sergeant. Help me! My arm is gone." I could hear screams from wounded and dying men all around us. I was overcome with my own thoughts of how to save our men. After all, I was the group's executive officer. From a few feet away, I heard our sergeant major yell out, "Major Jenkins, we've got to get the hell out of here!"

It was impossible for us to return fire. Any attempt to do so would draw the attention of the Japanese soldiers with deadly results. Our regiment couldn't advance and we couldn't stay there. The major had to devise a way to get us out of this hellhole. The Japanese had our range, and they were not letting up. I imagined Phil was thinking, "How in the hell did I lead my men into this? But more importantly, how do I get them out of here? I've got to stay calm." I recognized the look on my friend's face.

With trepidation, Major Jenkins turned back toward the trees bordering the killing field and motioned to his men to follow him. We began inching our way along as close to the ground as humanly possible. Knowing Phil as I did, he was probably thinking of his embarrassment at retreating in the face of enemy fire. Would he be court martialled we all wondered when we arrived in the safety of the trees? Now he probably knows how General Pickett must have felt at Gettysburg during the Civil War, I thought.

After many grueling minutes, I could see the major finally reach the woods, stand up and turn to see how our men were doing. I was close on his heels. The sergeants had things under control as much as possible and were urging their men to move quickly without endangering themselves. Our soldiers were dragging our dead and wounded comrades off the field while trying not to become casualties themselves. It was critical that the Japanese not know that we had turned and were retreating off the battlefield. If they discovered Major Jenkins' attempt to save his men, they could wipe out the American battalion with one quick attack. A few of our men had been killed in the maneuver, but most made it safely into the dense forest.

"Sergeant," I heard Phil shout. "Find Captain Beltrans and have him report to me immediately!"

"Yes sir," he replied.

I was the major's executive officer and his best friend. Phil rarely did anything without bouncing his idea off of me.

"And sergeant, have the men sit down and rest. We will be walking off again in a few minutes." The sergeant waved acknowledgement over his shoulder as he ran off to find me.

"Yes Phil. What's up?" I was out of breath but otherwise in good shape.

"Ray, do you remember the aerial photos the Air Corps guys showed us of this battlefield before the shooting started?"

"Yes, vaguely."

"As I recall, over here to our right is a shallow ravine, maybe just deep enough to hide a man crawling in it. It looked as if it extends all the way up the side of the mountain along the Japanese left flank. Our only chance for survival is to outflank these bastards. As we just discovered, hitting them head on means certain death for all of us, as we just discovered. You can see the ravine's entrance over there," Major Jenkins said pointing up the hill. He motioned to the sergeant major to join their conversation.

"Ray, the sergeant and I are going to take the lead and head up the ravine in single file. I want you to wait until all the men have moved out and then bring up the rear. When we reach the right spot, I will signal for us to stop. You will then be in charge of our left flank when we turn to our left and charge over the edge of the ravine toward the enemy."

"Rather like General Stonewall Jackson at the battle of Chancellorsville when the Union Army thought he was quitting the field and, instead, he hit their right flank and pushed them into a frantic retreat," I responded with a smile.

"Exactly Ray. Now let's move out. Sergeant, follow me!"

"Yes Sir."

I saw the major motion his battalion to stay low as they crawled their way up the ravine with the noisy battle raging to their left. I waited until the last man passed me and then turned to follow them up the ravine.

The ravine was getting shallower as it wandered up the hillside. Would we get to the right spot before some diligent Jap soldier spotted movement to his left and sounded the alarm? I was watching Phil carefully as he finally waved the column to a halt and motioned us to lie down and stay out of sight.

Turning to the left side of the small ravine, he crawled to the top and peered out over the edge. It was the site of a classic battlefield. The Japanese troops were spread out in front of him all directing their fire at the main battle line to his left. He was facing a completely exposed and undefended enemy left flank in front of him.

He saw Jap soldiers standing a hundred feet or so ahead pointing to the ground we had recently left. Obviously they had just discovered that there was no longer an enemy in front of them and were signaling their officers that the way was open for a coordinated charge straight into the Allied right flank, the area that had been Major Jenkins' responsibility to defend.

Phil slid back down to the bottom of the ravine, and I could see his animated gestures to his sergeant, "Tell the men to fix their bayonets and prepare for a charge. We're going to pull a Colonel Chamberlain on them; signal me when they are ready!"

I was always amazed at Phil's knowledge of battles fought in the past. An expert on military history, Phil loved to equate his movements with those of famous military leaders. His favorite hero was Lt. Colonel Joshua Chamberlain, commander of the Twentieth Maine Regiment at the battle of Gettysburg during the Civil War. Phil had often told me that he dreamed of the day when he could lead a bayonet charge against a surprised and unprepared enemy, therefore throwing the whole battle in his favor, as Colonel Chamberlain had done against General Longstreet's Confederate Army. Bayonet charges had lost their favor since the invention of the machine gun in WW I, but he thought this might be his chance to use it. I could see Phil checking his body for blood or other signs of wounds; he found none. He removed the half- empty magazine case from his Thompson and jammed in a full one. He didn't throw a cartridge into the breech for fear that the enemy would hear the sound. He needn't have worried. The noise of battle drowned out any sound a single soldier could make.

I watched the sergeant scurry back along the column toward me as the major watched his men fix their bayonets and look up at him with smiles. Some raised their fists in the air and turned ready to charge out of the ravine. At the far end of the line he could hear me yell "All's ready," at him.

It's now or never I thought.

TWO

I saw that Colonel Maruyama had set up his command post with care for his safety and for the control of his troops. I peeked up over the edge of the ravine and watched him continually scan the battlefield in front and down the slight incline that dropped off to the skirmish line.

He was surveying the line of battle around him with his binoculars and relayed orders to his units as the battle raged on. I knew from his reputation that he was a competent leader who had been in the China-Burma theatre for almost the entire war, and he knew that this battle for Myitkyina was the most critical fight he would wage. He had to take the airfield just ahead and then the town behind it. The battle had raged back and forth for weeks, but this was the climax. The colonel had thrown everything he had at the Allies to drive them out of Northern Burma, and we had faced the brunt of it.

Control of this critical town would determine who would be the masters of northern Burma, southern China and eastern India. Myitkyina was at the crossroads of the three countries, and success in this battle would be critical for the future of the Japanese Army in Southeast Asia and Colonel Maruyama's career. The Ledo Road went from India through Myitkyina on its way to China, and cutting this vital access would have significant effect on the ability of the Nationalist Chinese to stay in the war. Both sides needed to win.

I slid back into the ravine as I saw the colonel's gaze wander from straight ahead to his left. It then moved to the forest into which we has retreated, Then his body turned farther left toward us and the open plain behind our new position. He stared at what appeared to him to be a continual plain running from the combat area to the northwest. I peeked back over and heard him call his executive officer to his side. "Major, has anyone surveyed that area to our left to see if it could be used to launch an attack on our flank?"

I can only imagine the major's reply. "We have surveyed it sufficiently, Sir, to know that an attack from our left flank is not possible. However, we have troops continually watching that plain for a possible approach by the enemy."

The colonel nodded but did not reply. He stared for a moment to his left and then returned his concentration to the battle line in his front. He mulled at the meaning of the major's word "sufficiently," but too much was going on in front of him. His troops were advancing slowly, but steadily to the north, while pushing the Allied forces back against the airfield. I could see a smile creep over his face.

I later heard, that as we were preparing to attack, our officers at the Allied headquarters were pouring over maps as the American executive officer came running breathlessly into the tent. Lieutenant Colonel Edmonds shouted, "Colonel Stevenson, Major Jenkins has deserted his position on our right flank. There is nothing preventing Colonel Maruyama from overwhelming us from the west." Colonel Stevenson dropped his map and stepped out of his headquarters to scan his right flank with his binoculars. "My God colonel. You're right. Alert all commands to prepare for a pull back across the airfield."

THREE

As Colonel Maruyama stood at his command post, a location that allowed him to survey the entire battlefield, he could see what he presumed were the Allies beginning to pull back. He liked what he saw. He ordered his forward units on the left side to gather together and prepare to make a frontal assault that would insure the victory he had so long craved.

As we crawled to the top of the ravine, we could see his normal scowl turn into a rare grin as he contemplated his victorious march into the Burmese town. This was the time for us to move, and Phil, sensing the same thing, screamed at us to charge at full speed.

The Japanese colonel suddenly heard shouts and automatic rifle fire to his left. He turned in time to see almost three hundred American soldiers wildly charging over a small ridge at his left flank, a flank he had heard was in no danger. He looked back at his unit but saw an inadequate number of troops prepared to repulse an attack from that quarter.

He could suddenly see that his well-planned attack was about to collapse around him. Why had he listened to his exec? He turned to his staff, which was standing with their mouths open looking at their left flank. With no small amount of anger, he shouted, "Let's pack up and get the hell out of here." His face turned a bright red.

Major Jenkins led the charge on the American right flank while I was shouting and leading from our left. We were all tired of being kicked around, and our anger and frustration showed as we ran down the slope to the surprised and terrified Japanese soldiers.

Our troops fired a few rounds and then resorted to using their bayonets. I could see the Japanese turn and flee in terror as armies that have been outflanked have done for centuries. I could see that Phil was holding his fire except when necessary, and concentrating on leading his men. We were all astonished at the young age of the Japanese soldiers. Most were in their teens, and few were trained well enough to defend themselves in hand-to-hand combat. The bayonet is a terrible weapon, I thought, as I heard the screams of the dying and wounded Japanese soldiers.

Our American soldiers showed no mercy, and no one was about to suggest that they give any. But I saw slaughter like I had never seen before. Teen-age boys were screaming in terror as bayonets were thrust into their stomachs. The entire left flank of the Japanese Army rolled up and fled, dropping their rifles because they could run faster without them. As they ran, bayonets came in through their backs.

The battlefield was now a hell of crying, screaming and dying soldiers, mostly Japanese. Their officers started first, turning away from the battle and running for safety. Then their soldiers followed. The ground was covered with blood, but our troops, like sharks smelling blood in the water, ran fast enough to kill everyone they could reach, attacking some who were already dead.

I found out later that our field commander, Colonel Stevenson, was throwing files and weapons into a truck bed as fast as he could thinking that our position had collapsed. He was shouting at his staff to "move it," and "let's get the hell out of here fast." What in the hell had caused his best field officer, Major Jenkins, to evacuate his position on the Army's right flank and leave it vulnerable to Japanese counter attack?

He had just finished packing and had swung his legs into the front seat of his personal jeep when he heard a shout from behind. He was tempted to ignore it. Time was running out. But he looked back to see Sergeant Haskell waving his arms and shouting. "No colonel.

Don't leave. Wait!" The sergeant was running at top speed toward the colonel's jeep with his M-I carbine slung over his shoulder.

"What the hell?" The colonel was in no mood to wait for a sergeant who probably just wanted a ride out of the battle area.

Out of breath, the sergeant stumbled up to the jeep. "Colonel! You have got to see this. Get out sir and come to that rise over there and look back to the battle line; bring your binoculars. Please sir."

The colonel stood out of breath from the short climb trying to focus his binoculars on the hillside in front of him. "My God! What's happening?" There was a band of maybe three hundred soldiers running at top speed toward the Japanese charging their left flank and screaming bloody murder. The excitement surged inside him as he recognized the banner of Major Jenkins regiment leading the killing and pushing the enemy troops in disarray back into the jungle. The Japanese troops were leaving their weapons on the ground and their dead and wounded at the mercy of the Americans. He could see Major Jenkins in the lead waving his men forward in the style of a classic Civil War charge. I was located on our unit's left flank trying to control the charge from the left in the midst of bloody chaos.

A friend of mine who was there later told me that with all the calmness and dignity that he could muster, Colonel Stevenson turned to his staff that had now joined him on the rise. "All right, who authorized Major Jenkins to pull out of his assigned position and charge the enemy from their left flank?" He looked at his officers expecting an answer, but got nothing but shrugs. After a few moments of silence, Sergeant Haskell said from the rear of the group, "Sir, no one gave him permission. He made this move on his own initiative." As they all watched the remaining Japanese forces running away in terror, the sergeant added, "A move, I might add, that has saved the day for us." Only a battle hardened sergeant could have answered the colonel like that.

Out of breath, I saw Phil stop to look around. He had been wounded, but not seriously. As he surveyed the terrible scene around him, looking at the battlefield's dead and dying, his eye suddenly stopped on a wounded Japanese soldier lying on the ground in front of him and pointing his rifle at him. I quickly raised my carbine and fired at the Japanese soldier, but it was too late. I heard the soldier's rifle fire as Phil grabbed his chest and collapse in a pool of blood.

FOUR

I awoke with a start when the pilot announced that we were now arriving at the Myitkyina airport. I remember the jar of the flaps being deployed and then the thud of the landing gear dropping into its extended position. I rubbed my eyes and looked out toward the southeast horizon where I could make out the mountains in the haze where Phil and I had lived for so many months.

To my left I saw the Yunnan Province of China. Looking straight down, I could see the magnificent Irrawaddi River, now called the Ayeyarwady, meandering through its flood plain in central Burma. The Irrawaddi has always been the lifeblood of the country starting in the Himalayas and flowing more than a thousand miles south before emptying into the Andaman Sea south of Rangoon.

We were now circling over the town that the Allies had liberated from the Japanese in one of the most ferocious battles fought in South East Asia during the war. I didn't know what I expected to see when I left the plane, but it would be nothing like what I had seen back in September of 1945.

As I walked out of the airport, I recognized nothing that I saw around me. It was somewhere near here that I, Major Jenkins and our men stopped the big Japanese counter offensive in the summer of 1944. It was bloody, but Merrill's Marauders and our allies prevailed; the Japanese forces were driven back and the city of Myitkyina was saved. I looked around, and hailed a waiting taxi.

When I strolled into the lobby of my hotel, I was amazed by its beauty and modern architecture. The employees were very nice, and I loved my room with its view of the river and the mountains beyond.

It had been thirty-five years since my friend Phil Jenkins and I had fought to keep this town free from the Japanese, but it felt like it was only yesterday.

I had invited her, but my wife wasn't interested in coming with me half way around the world to see the battlefield on which we had fought. She preferred to stay at home with our grandchildren. So I decided to come alone and visit for the first time the country in which we had fought. I looked in the mirror and saw a middle-aged man staring back at me. I was now someone who could never survive the extreme hardships, the jungle and the conflict that we all had endured.

I had always felt guilty that I survived the war while so many of my buddies had not. I knew that this was a feeling that many returning service men experienced after the war. Phil's wife had kept in touch with me knowing that I was her husband's best friend. She had re-married in 1947 and raised Phil's girls in a way that would have made him very proud. Janice and I had exchanged Christmas cards every year sharing pictures of Phil's girls through graduation and marriage. Now Phil had grandkids of his own, but he was not around to enjoy them.

Phil's wife had encouraged me to go to Burma, to take pictures of Phil's grave and of the country in which the 5307th had lived for almost four years. Janice thought it would be good for his grandkids to see where their grandfather was buried in the country we had fought so hard to liberate from the Japanese.

I had returned to my native Santa Fe, New Mexico when I finally left India in 1945. My ancestors had settled the American Southwest coming from Mexico in the seventeenth century, and I had no intention of leaving it. I had made it big in business after the war, which only increased my guilt that my good friend from California had not lived to do the same. But now I was tired from the long trip and just wanted some rest. I barely remember removing my shoes before I fell asleep on top of the covers.

FIVE

waking early as was my custom ever since my days in the Army, I started to dress and then realized that I was already dressed. After putting on my shoes and brushing my teeth, I walked down stairs in time for a hearty breakfast, happy to be served an American style breakfast in my hotel. I hadn't eaten rice for thirty years and didn't intend to start now.

I stepped out into the morning sun and hailed a waiting cab. After settling in the back seat, I asked politely, "Please take me to the American Memorial Cemetery near the old Army hospital." The driver nodded seeming to understand exactly where I wanted to go.

I watched the magnificent Irrawaddi pass by as we drove along its edge. It was still muddy, just as I had remembered it, bringing back a stream of memories as I stared out the window. The cab finally turned into the memorial grounds with its beautifully kept lawn that seemed to go on forever. I stepped out, paid the driver and thanked him. The driver smiled, waved good-bye and drove off. I turned and looked out across the huge cemetery.

I walked over to the building where the buried American troops would be listed. "Can you tell me where the 5307th, the Merrill's Marauders, are buried, miss?" She smiled, opened up a map of the cemetery and laid it on the counter. Fortunately, it was in English.

I walked slowly over the grounds in the direction that the lady had pointed. I was studying the map as I progressed through the gravesites of many young American soldiers. There were also British,

Indian, Chinese and Chindit names on the grave markers. My heart beat faster. Did I really want to do this?

Finally I stood in the middle of the 5307th, looking at

I stopped at each grave, remembering how I had trained the young soldiers to kill and to survive in this hostile environment. The worst problem that they faced was the monsoon rains that caused diseases and so much of their misery. I remembered our troubles all too well as I walked up to each stone marker, snapped to attention, gave a salute and paid my respects.

I then said something personal that I remembered about each man. "Corporal O'Malley. I warned you to stop smoking or it would kill you." Smiling, I recalled that living a long life I Burma wasn't an option.

As I travelled among the markers, my sadness and anger grew. "Why did these brave young men have to die? And for what?" I wiped away another tear.

After spending a few minutes, I walked to the next grave. Then I saw it. Phillip W. Jenkins, Major U.S. Army, Born Aug. 17, 1915, Died Sept. 3, 1945. I finally raised my head and saw a bench a few feet away. I walked over and sat down staring out across the Irrawaddi.

SIX

I watched him intently as the cool water felt good running over his hand while Major Jenkins filled his canteen from the small stream trickling down the mountain. He stood slightly downstream as it filled, so that the sweat dripping off his forehead would not end up in his drinking water. He was almost getting accustomed to the hot muggy air that permeated the jungle in this part of Burma, but this monsoon pattern was getting him down. It had started only a few weeks ago at the beginning of May; the sun was out now, but probably only briefly. The stifling jungle air seemed to be as heavy with water as it was with bugs. Whenever the sun came out, the major ordered his men to take off their clothes so their skin could dry out before the next storm hit.

Major Jenkins screwed the cap back on his canteen, slipped it into its belt container and turned to walk over to a rock. As he sat down, he took off his shirt and set it next to his backpack and submachine gun that were leaning against a tree. The sun felt good on his bare back even though its heat added to the jungle air temperature. He closed his eyes in hopes of getting a couple of minutes of rest before his combat team had to push on up the winding jungle trail.

Just as he was about to doze off, he heard his sergeant major say, "Hey major I don't think that snake crawling up your leg is poisonous."

The major jumped up, pulled his .45 automatic from its holster, cocked it and spun around all in one motion while pointing his weapon down at the rock he had just been leaning against. As his eyes focused, he could see that there was nothing there but sticks, while he heard the men around him break into laughter.

They knew that he was deathly afraid of snakes, and there were plenty of them in Burma. It seemed to him that the worst ones were all living next to the trail his men had been walking along since they left India.

He released the hammer on his .45, slid it back into its holster and sat down; now he was wide-awake. He closed his eyes again, but sleep was no longer an option as his mind filled with the thoughts that often envelop a commanding officer. The major loved the men who served under him, especially his sergeant major and the other senior enlisted men in his unit. They were the remnants of what had been known as the 5307th

Vinegar Joe, as General Stilwell was affectionately called, reported to the British Admiral, Lord Louis Mountbatten, the supreme commander in the India, Burma, and China region. At least that was the way it was intended to work. Unfortunately for the chain of command, General Joe seldom took the time to get permission from Louis or even keep him informed of his plans of attacking the Japanese. Lord Mountbatten often heard what was happening in Stilwell's army by reading about it in the local newspaper.

Major Jenkins' command had been sent into the jungle to find what was left of the Japanese Army that had escaped from the battle of Myitkyina. His unit was made up mostly of convicts recruited from prisons by the promise of freedom if they "volunteered" for duty in General Merrill's command. They were originally trained at Deogarth, India, in hand-to-hand combat, learning how to kill the enemy with knives, machetes, firearms and their bare hands if necessary. They were trained to live behind enemy lines and to survive in the jungle terrain of northern Burma and southern China. They were good at killing Japanese with resignation if not pleasure.

As he was lying in the warm sun, he reviewed the events that brought him to this part of the world. It was just over a year ago that he and his men had fought what was probably the most intense and important battle of the Burma campaign, the battle of Myitkyina.

It began when the Allied troops arrived at the airbase. The Japanese fought bravely to capture this important trade route and road junction town on the Irrawaddy River.

Led by Katchin scouts, 2750 of Merrill's Marauders, had marched more than 1000 miles from India, entering Burma through the Patkai Region over the Himalaya Mountains, all behind Japanese lines. Our troops completely surprised the entrenched enemy and hit their larger force with a ferocity that the Japanese never expected. Unfortunately, our smaller American force had been depleted by various jungle diseases contracted along our march into Burma. Two of the worst came from drinking bad water and sleeping in the jungle mud.

In addition, Merrill's Marauders, and especially Major Jenkins' small command, had suffered from a problem to which no World War II Army unit should have been subjected. Food rations were inappropriate for use behind enemy lines. Some desk officer in India had decided that the army that was operating behind the Japanese could survive on K-rations alone. K-rations provided only 2830 calories per day, an amount that could not support a soldier in the field in a war. But worst of all, K-rations were only partially edible, and the hungry soldiers threw much of their food away. Our men made up for their poor rations by trading their cigarettes and K-rations to the accompanying Chinese soldiers and Burmese civilians for eggs, chickens and other local delicacies. I often saw Phil's temper rise when he thought about the rations the Army had given our men.

However, unknown to most civilians back home, disease was the worst problem that our soldiers faced. The terrible weather was bad enough, but even worse was the amoebic dysentery that struck the men as they marched along their thousand-mile route. I remembered that this killer arrived with the two Chinese divisions that were sent to aid the Americans in their attack on Myitkyina. It seems that our troops picked up dysentery from the Chinese who used the adjacent river as a toilet. Unfortunately, our troops used the same river as their drinking water supply. The Chinese boiled their water before drinking, but our guys did not.

Scrub typhus was just as deadly and was caused by sleeping in the mud. Both diseases took a heavy toll on us as we marched into Burma. We wondered if the home folks would ever be told of how many soldiers died of the diseases found here in Southeast Asia.

SEVEN

The battle for Myitkyina began in May 1944, and continued until August when two Chinese divisions were flown in for reinforcements. Fighting with the Americans, they swung the battle in favor of the Allied forces. Often our unit helped slaughter hundreds of Japanese troops in hand-to-hand fighting in a brilliant flanking maneuver. Only a few hundred enemy troops escaped the carnage. Regrettably, the Japanese commanding officer, Colonel Maruyama, escaped with almost three-hundred men. The escaping enemy troops fled up into the mountainous jungle of northern Burma to lick their wounds and prepare for future mischief. Phil was badly injured in the battle while leading his combat unit in a savage counter attack after feigning a retreat. His initiative helped trap and kill a large number of Japanese troops before they could escape.

Phil remembered a sudden, sharp pain in his leg and chest and then felt a solid thud on the side of his head just as he passed out. Although badly wounded, the event probably saved his life. The next thing he knew, he was awake in a field hospital several miles behind the front lines in a great deal of pain. He didn't stay awake long but floated in and out of consciousness until the medic finally gave him a shot that knocked him out for several days. No one had told him yet that most of his combat unit had been killed in their brave and murderous attack on the Japanese flank.

I had not been injured in the attack; so I was in charge of getting Phil to a field hospital and rounding up the remainder of our group.

There weren't many left who were uninjured and most were sent back to India, but I received permission to stay at the hospital watching my friend.

When the major finally woke up a few days later, he noticed that a combat medal of some kind had been pinned to his hospital pajamas. The pinning had probably been done by some staff officer who had been ordered to come through the ward and pass out jewelry to improve the morale of the dying soldiers. No, there were two medals on his chest. One was obviously the Purple Heart; he could tell by its shape. The other was one that he did not immediately recognize. He studied its red, white and blue vertical stripes and bright star from an upside-down position. When a medic walked by, Phil rose up slowly on his elbows and asked him what it was. The medic walked over, smiled and said, "Major, that is the Silver Star, given to you yesterday by General Merrill himself. Turn it over and read the inscription on the back."

I was sitting near his bed, but he couldn't see me. He was having a hard time focusing on the small printing. "For Gallantry in Action," it read.

For the first time in two weeks, the pain in his head didn't matter as I saw tears fill his eyes and run down his cheeks. He rolled his head over against the pillow and fell back to sleep thinking about his men who probably hadn't survived. It was several days before he woke again. The medals were still there.

EIGHT

It was time for Phil to stop thinking about the past and get his men up and back on the trail. The major still had slight pain in the side of his head when he moved it suddenly. The doctor had told him that he would probably experience that pain for the rest of his life. He would get used to it. "Sure I will," he would often say to me sarcastically. "Doctors have a way of telling their patients that their pain is not serious. I never heard a doctor say that about his own pain.

"Sergeant, get the men moving please." He was always polite when issuing an order to his men. They seemed to appreciate it and would always work a bit harder when they were shown a little respect. He felt that the respect he showed his men in no way compromised his authority, because he could be a terror when he suspected that someone was not doing his job or failed to show respect to him. No one wanted to get the major angry. Plus they knew they were being led by a genuine hero and a wounded one at that.

He rose slowly from his resting spot against the rock, put his arms through his backpack, raised it into position and slung his submachine gun over his shoulder. Soldiers standing close to him would offer to help him get "loaded up," but he would only reply with a good natured scowl and insist that he could "do it himself." The whole process was more important to his machismo than anything else, and the major was not going to let his age or wounds prevent him from keeping up with his younger soldiers. Actually he wasn't that much older than his men; his wounds just made him feel older.

It was typically my job to lead the men through the jungle. A dedicated group of younger machete-wielding solders followed me closely and continuously hacked their way along the overgrown trail. The major and his sergeant major brought up the rear. He liked it that way because by the time he got to any place on the trail, it had been completely cleared by the bushwhacking soldiers ahead of him. I had developed a well-deserved reputation for leading our men through the enemy-infested jungles. Occasionally, we would stumble on a lone Japanese sentry, or perhaps two, who I quickly dispatched with my razor sharp bowie knife.

I was never without my beloved bowie knife, a throwback from growing up in New Mexico. When I was a boy, my grandfather spent hours teaching me how to use the knife with amazing efficiency. Major Jenkins remembered the times when, bringing up the rear, he would look down beside the trail and see a Japanese soldier with a slit throat or no head at all. He knew that I had been doing my job.

Everything we did on that trip had to be accomplished without a sound, to avoid arousing the enemy, including, and especially, killing Japanese soldiers. So far, we had been so effective at this that Colonel Maruyama had no idea that there was an enemy nearby in the jungle, and the major wanted to keep it that way.

The major's aide brought his hammock up and asked him where he would like it strung. "Surprise me corporal. I want a good night's sleep after that trek we made today, and I will leave its location up to you."

It wasn't long before he was stretched out in his new hammock resting his almost-healed legs and sore head. Our team of officers gathered around him to see if he had any orders or wanted to discuss plans for tomorrow's walk. "Let's don't talk now men. Go crawl into your hammocks and we will meet first thing in the morning and review the upcoming day." Everyone let out a restrained sigh of relief and said, "Yes sir," in unison and walked off happily to their safe but somewhat public bedrooms.

NINE

As we lay in our hammocks, my thoughts drifted back to the field hospital and Phil's slow but steady recovery from his wounds. I remembered noticing that wounded soldiers around him, some of whom had received worse wounds than he, had been bandaged up and put on flights back to India. In fact, the ward he was in was almost empty. He was sitting up finishing his hospital breakfast one morning when in walked Colonel Charles Hunter, the new commanding officer of Merrill's Marauders. The startled major tried to sit at attention, but that didn't work. The colonel smiled and raised his hand. "It will be a while yet before you can stand or sit at attention major. May I sit next to you while you finish your breakfast?" I moved out of my chair to give the colonel a place to sit next to Phil's bed.

"Of course colonel," he replied wondering why the colonel wanted to talk to him. He knew that finishing his breakfast while it was hot was no longer an option.

The colonel wasted no time. "As you may know major, General Merrill has been relieved of his command and I am now the C.O. of Merrill's Marauders."

"Yes sir."

"He had his second heart attack a few days ago, and Central Command felt that a change in command was necessary for his health and for the benefit of the 5307th."

The major nodded.

"Unfortunately, the 5307th was so decimated in the battle for Myitkyani that it no longer exists as a fighting unit. The few hundred men left were almost all wounded in the battle or sick from local diseases. They have all been sent back to India for rest and recuperation, except for you and your friend Captain Beltrans here. When they recover, they will be incorporated into existing units to provide experienced fighters along side the new recruits we are getting." The colonel paused to consider the effect on the major, "Yes, the 5307th is history, except for one unit. Yours!!!"

The major looked around the room and his glance stopped at me, but there was no one else in the room from our unit.

"However, let me back up. You may have heard that over three hundred Japs escaped into the jungle with their commanding officer, Colonel Maruyama. As well as we fought, we unfortunately did not get all of them." Phil thought that the use of "we" was interesting. "They headed up into the mountains southeast of here and have not been seen since, at least not by us. They have, however, become very conspicuous to the local Burmese civilians who are living in the mountains. We have reports of bloody massacres occurring in the small villages and towns in the hills in which Colonel Maruyama and his band of killers now live. Apparently, his aim is to cause as much havoc and civilian deaths as possible in Northern Burma. There are no troops to oppose him, so it appears his only goal is to kill as many innocent civilians as he can before the war ends. Unfortunately, we have no troops to spare to go after him."

The colonel's intent was slowly becoming clear to Phil, but he made no comment.

"As I am sure you are beginning to realize, this is where you come in."

Ignoring Phil's sarcasm, the colonel continued. "We have taken the liberty of selecting and organizing an elite group of dedicated soldiers who would rather kill Japanese than go home. I believe there are about one hundred-fifty of them. They have been brought together here, but they need final training in jungle warfare led by a brave and experienced jungle fighter like you. They have been flown into the airport now for your inspection. Of course, the final training will be your responsibility."

"The doctors say that you will need a little longer to recuperate and then they're all yours," the colonel said as he rose and shook Phil's hand. "My training officer, Captain Mc Neil here will give you the support and help that you need. Don't be afraid to ask him. Remember, we are counting on you to get Colonel Maruyama and his men by whatever means you think necessary. No questions will be asked."

"Colonel, I have only one request, that you give me Captain Beltrans here to be my executive officer. I can't do this without him." I remember smiling at Phil for his compliment.

"That's fine with me major" He turned to the officer next to him. "See to it captain."

"Jolly good show then, as our English friends would say," as the colonel rose and walked briskly out of the ward followed by his staff in order of their rank. Only Captain McNeil remained.

"Shall we get started sir?" he asked Major Jenkins with a smile. The major returned his smile and turned to his now cold breakfast. "When I finish my breakfast captain."

TEN

The rain had stopped, but the sky remained overcast covering the troops with a starless night. The major kept his tarp draped over him just in case. He could hear the snoring of the men nearest him and the sounds of animals in the still night air. His eyes were slowly closing when he heard a soft rustle in the bushes on the trail they had just traveled. He knew there was a sentry sitting out there, so he had no fear that an enemy was crawling toward them. Besides, what would be out in this jungle in the dark other than an animal? Then he heard it again a bit louder. The major softly slipped on his shoes and rolled out of his hammock and onto the ground making no sound. Staring in the direction of the sound did not help. Nothing is as black and visually impenetrable as the jungle on a moonless night.

He began to crawl slowly toward the trail checking that his .45 was still in its holster on his belt. He was startled when he brushed against Lieutenant Schultz now moving beside him. The two officers reached the trail together and then strained to hear whatever was out there. In a couple of minutes they both heard a movement in the brush again. Where is our sentry, the major wondered? Now the sound was closer, almost within reach. The lieutenant reached into his pocket, quietly pulled out a good-sized flashlight and pointed it in the direction of the sound. The major gently reached up and pulled his arm back. He wanted to verify what he heard one more time. Now the sound was louder, like a person trying to muffle a sneeze.

The two officers jumped up, the major pulled out his pistol, and the lieutenant flipped on his flashlight. No sneezing Jap soldier was going to surprise them! There he was, curled up under a bush trying to avoid the light now shining in his face. The lieutenant spoke first.

"That's no Jap soldier, sir," he said as the major re- holstered his weapon and reached down to pick up what appeared to be a frightened little boy. Now lights blinked on all around them as soldiers in various stages of undress came running up. In a few seconds, their Burmese scout pushed his way through the group and moved up next to the major, firing a stream of unintelligible Burmese words at the intruder. The boy looked down at the ground, shivering with fright. The scout repeated his questioning, and the boy finally responded in a weak voice that was barely audible. They spoke back and forth for a few minutes in Burmese, and the scout turned to the major.

"This is not a boy major. This is a young Burmese woman who lives in the local village. She heard us marching along the trail this afternoon, decided to follow and perhaps steal some food. She hasn't eaten for days." She looked up at her captors with tears running down her cheeks.

"I would like to question her. Ask her if we feed her, will she stay around until morning so we can talk," the major said. The scout smiled. "Don't worry major. She is terrified of the animals that move around in the jungle at night. She will definitely be here in the morning."

"Lieutenant, please get this woman all the food she wants, and find her a dry place to sleep. And you will answer to me if she is gone in the morning. By the way, find out why our sentry allowed her to sneak past him without warning us or stopping her. Let's all get back to sleep now. We have a big day tomorrow."

The woman looked up at Major Jenkins as if she understood his order and thanked him in a language he could not understand.

ELEVEN

A s the sun broke over the eastern mountains, the major, our other six officers, Burmese scout and senior sergeants all sat around the jungle clearing in a circle facing the little Burmese women who had crawled into our camp the night before. Phil, sipping his second cup of coffee, rubbed the sleep out of his eyes. Addressing his scout, "Does she have a name?"

"She refers to herself as Nang, a rather common name in this region of Burma sir."

"Hmmm. Ask her where we are and if there are any Japanese soldiers in this area."

After several minutes of intense Burmese conversation, the scout turned to the major.

"Your question hit a sore spot with her sir. She is roaming these hills because a Japanese raiding party raped and tortured everyone in her village, and then killed them all. She says they accused her people of helping the American forces, but there are no American soldiers for hundreds of miles around except us.

"She said that she was at the river getting water when the attack started, and she escaped by hiding in the jungle until the Japs left, taking all the food they could carry. She returned to the village and buried her parents and sisters the best she could and then fled when she heard the soldiers returning. Sir, she wants to know if she could have a gun and travel with us until we find them and then let her do the killing. She said she can still see the look on their faces as the Japanese soldiers mutilated her baby sisters, family and friends."

I remember that no one in the group moved or spoke. They looked down at the ground and squeezed their weapons, some finally kicking the mud. A few wiped their eyes with the back of their sleeves, probably coming as close as they ever came to crying. Everyone waited for the major to reply. Finally he coughed, rubbed his growing beard, and without responding to her request, said in a soft voice, completely unlike him, "Ask her if she knows where the Japanese camp is located," as his words trailed off.

After a few minutes of back and forth exchange in a language which the men were slowly beginning to understand, he turned to the major, "Well, first, she wants to know why you did not respond to her request, and second, she said that she could lead us to the enemy camp, but only if you give her one of our tommy guns with ammo."

The men all grinned and looked at the major wondering how he would respond to being blackmailed by a young Burmese woman. Phil looked down at his tommy gun resting against his knee and smiled as he thought that that it was almost as big as Nang. This is a pretty tough woman, he thought. "Tell her that she may accompany us and when we encounter the Japs, we will let her do her share of killing with whatever weapon she can handle." He thought his non-committal answer might serve the purpose.

We all turned to Nang wondering if she would accept the major's response and lead us to the enemy camp. She was obviously not happy as the scout relayed the major's proposal. She looked down at her hands as she contemplated her options, but she knew that if she were to repay the horrors that the Japanese troops had inflicted on her village, she might have to compromise, at least for now. She nodded. Our men all smiled in agreement.

"So what does she know about the enemy's location," I asked.

The scout turned back after a minute's conversation and said, "Nang says that there is an enemy outpost about five miles ahead that the Japanese use to warn their headquarters of hostile forces that might be coming along this trail. Their main base is located on that mountain over there," pointing toward the southeast. "She says that there may be twenty or so soldiers in the outpost and they have a radio that keeps them in contact with the main camp."

"How far beyond the outpost is the main Japanese camp?'

"She says she does not know exactly, but it's probably a good couple of days march."

"She has heard from local sources that there are around 300, maybe slightly more."

"That sounds like Colonel Maruyama's escapees to me," I said.

"Yes it does, but unfortunately we have about half that many troops," the major jumped in. "Let's think about a way to draw them out and even the odds a bit." Everyone nodded.

"Major, Nang just told me that she can lead us on a trail that goes around the outpost up ahead, but without the mules. As quiet as they try to be, the Japs on guard will probably hear them. The rest of us could make it without being detected."

"Lieutenant Briggs, you will remain here with the mule train and their guards. Do not move from this location until you hear from me. The rest of us will proceed around the Jap outpost and decide what to do next. Is that clear to everyone?"

"Yes sir." We all jumped up and continued walking along the trail.

TWELVE

After following Nang quietly around the outpost and about a half a mile beyond it, we all sat down to rest in a small jungle clearing. It had been raining heavily as we walked, and the water seemed to turn to steam when it hit the hot ground. The smell and humidity were intense, as was the concern felt by Major Jenkins as he sat on a log. He was leading a crack outfit of trained fighters, who in later years would be called "Rangers," and he was within striking distance of his archenemy, Colonel Maruyama, whom he had been tracking for months. But we knew that the Japanese force had the upper hand.

They were larger, higher up on the mountain, experienced and spoiling for a fight. The only advantage Major Jenkins had was that the Japanese did not know that we were in the area, or at least that is what Phil hoped. If only he could coax the three hundred or so Japanese troops off their mountaintop and into a trap! But how do you trap a force of three hundred enemy troops experienced in jungle fighting? The fact that it had finally stopped raining did not improve his mood.

After a hard fight with a band of local mosquitoes, and then a few minutes staring down at the ground, the troops heard a commotion coming down the trail. The men all turned in the direction of the noise, cocked their weapons and waited patiently. They turned back to eating their snacks when they saw me running down the trail. When I spotted the major, I stopped and waved at him to follow me back up the trail. I had been scouting up ahead and had seen something that I thought might interest my friend.

I saw Phil raise his aching body, pick up his weapon, stretch and walk toward me. "This better be good, Ray" he said. He soon caught up with me and we continued walking side by side along the trail.

"You have got to see this, Phil!" As we walked along, the terrain around the trail began to slope upward to the right and downward to the left toward the small creek that we had been following for several days. We were still traveling through heavy jungle, and visibility was limited. After walking about two hundred yards, we broke out into a large clearing, which allowed us to see ahead for a good distance. We stopped to survey the surrounding countryside.

"Look Phil. The trail turns left and heads down the hill for a short distance crosses the small creek we have been following, and then climbs up the other side. It then turns right, continuing to follow the creek, and running along the opposite side of the gully, the side on which there are no trees."

Phil noticed that as the trail progressed following the creek up the ravine, it passed along a canyon wall. Someone had dug into a steep mountain cliff to build this trail many years ago. Once on the trail, you could not go right or left, only straight ahead. As he stared at the scenery in front of him, his heart jumped as he realized what I was showing him. There was no jungle on that side of the gully, only a bare mountainside along which the trail passed. There was no cover for anyone walking along the trail until it returned into the jungle several hundred yards ahead. He turned his gaze to the side of the gully on which he and I were still standing. His heart jumped again! Our side of the gully was covered with thick jungle foliage.

He looked around at my smiling face, slapped me on the back as a football coach would slap his star quarterback after he had just made the winning touchdown. "You are a smart man captain. Remind me to promote you to major when we get home," Phil exclaimed.

But there was still one problem. Did the exposed trail extend far enough so that all three hundred Japanese soldiers would be exposed on it at once? It would not do to have several dozen of them still in the jungle at the other end when the fighting started. "How far does this open trail extend before it disappears back into the jungle, Ray?

"I walked its length before I came back to get you Phil, and I would say that three hundred soldiers would fit on it very nicely, that is assuming that they are not strung out too far," I replied.

"Okay. Go back to the men, interrupt their rest and bring them all up here. I'll plan our next move while I wait. And by the way, be sure and bring Sergeant Hashimoto with you. He will be an important part of this ambush."

Sergeant Hashimoto was a second generation Japanese American born and raised in the San Francisco Bay area. He spoke nothing but Japanese while growing up and only spoke English when he learned it in school. His parents owned a small grocery store that supplied food to the surrounding community, but they all had been rounded up and sent to an internment camp in the spring of 1942. Sergeant Hashimoto was one of the first Japanese Americans to enlist in the army, offering his language skills to prove his loyalty to his parents' adopted country. His ability to speak Japanese had proven to be very useful to Merrill's Marauders on several occasions.

His most famous exploit happened during a battle that had led up to the battle of Myitkyina. The fighting was extremely bitter, and the Allies were overwhelming a battalion of Japanese troops. When it became clear that the Allied troops had the upper hand, the Japanese, trying to escape the slaughter, turned and fled back toward the jungle. Seeing that they might lose an important chance to wipe out a big part of the enemy force, Sergeant Hashimoto jumped out of his foxhole and ran along the enemy's flank in the direction they were retreating. He stopped, and shouted as loud as he could ordering them in fluent Japanese to return to the battle because a battalion of Japanese infantry was on its way and would soon reinforce their beleaguered battalion. The Japanese troops, thinking that this was their commanding officer ordering them back into battle, turned and charged back toward the Allied lines. But, of course, there were no reinforcements, and the entire battalion was wiped out. Sergeant Hashimoto was given the bronze star and promoted to master sergeant for his heroic action that had resulted in the death of hundreds of enemy soldiers.

THIRTEEN

The sun was now out in full force and was raising spirits as our unit gathered around the major to hear what scheme he had come up with now. "All right men look around you and tell me what you see," the major said as we all sat down in the clearing.

"An exposed trail that extends maybe three hundred yards along the north edge of the creek," responded one soldier.

"Good. Now give me another name for what you are looking at."

"A shooting gallery," a voice from the rear answered. The men laughed.

"Exactly corporal, a shooting gallery. A gallery that, if we can lure the Japanese to it, will spell their doom." The soldiers looked at each other with satisfied grins. The Burmese scout sitting next to Nang softly translated the major's words so she could be a part of the discussion. She smiled too.

"But we have a problem don't we major?" Lieutenant Schultz spoke up without much conviction.

"Yes, we do lieutenant. Why don't you tell us what it is?"

"How do you get three hundred Japanese soldiers to walk down a trail that exposes their flank to murderous gunfire?" He now felt more confident. The men all nodded in agreement.

The soldiers talked softly among themselves waving their hands and pointing at the trail. No one spoke up.

The scout raised his hand slowly hoping that the major would not see him. "Yes, what does our scout have to say?" The major was embarrassed because he could never remember the scout's Burmese name

"Nang wants me to tell you that it is not as big a problem as you make it out to be, Sir" He added the "sir" that she had left out. "She says that the Japanese will always rush to reinforce one of their garrisons that is under siege." He stopped and looked back at her waiting for her to continue.

"Of course Sir, that's the answer to the big question," I jumped in. "We attack the outpost and then wait for the main enemy force to come to their aid. We ambush them as they march down the trail over there." A murmur of agreement went around the group. "That is a tactic as old as the Spartans."

"Yes, captain, we have not invented it here, but I think you have identified the attack plan very well. There is more to it that that. We have got to make the colonel believe that he must relieve his outpost with his entire force at once. If our attack is too weak, the outpost will be able to hold on by itself. If the attack is too strong, he will not waste his troops on a failed effort. Sergeant Hashimoto! This is where you come in."

The sergeant was sitting near the edge of the group listening intently and trying to picture how he might fit into the plans. A smile came over his face when he heard the major call his name. "Yes Sir?"

"Sergeant, you have to play the Hollywood role here like you have never played before. It will be up to you to convince the colonel up on top of that mountain over there that he must send all of his troops to rescue his small force that will be under attack by us. But they must not know that our attack group is part of a larger American force waiting in the jungle beside the trail. Lieutenant Schultz."

"You will be in overall command of the attack on the outpost and you will coordinate everything you do with Sergeant Hashimoto. Do not wipe them out too quickly, and do everything necessary to make the group at the outpost think that you are local Burmese civilians trying to get even for some previous massacre carried out by the colonel's men. Do you understand lieutenant?"

"But you, Sergeant Hashimoto, will have the toughest job of all. When the sun sets this evening, I want you to crawl up to the radio shack located at the rear of the compound, listen to the radio operator and familiarize yourself with the way he talks to his headquarters. There will obviously be some code words that he uses which will tell the colonel that the operator is legitimate. Memorize the code, because after the lieutenant and his men here have been fighting for about thirty minutes, I want you to move quietly into the radio shack, kill the Japanese operator and take over transmission of his radio. If he hasn't yet asked for help, that will be your first assignment on the radio. If he has already asked for help, you must confirm his request and beg the colonel to rescue his men quickly, because they are being slaughtered in front of you. Do you understand, sergeant?"

"Are there any questions? Lieutenant Schultz. I want you to open your attack tomorrow morning at 0600 hours exactly. Is that clear?"

Before the lieutenant could answer, Phil continued, "The rest of us will spread out on the jungle covered bank where we are sitting now. Set up the camouflaged machine guns about forty yards apart, and Captain Beltrans will open fire just before the lead Jap troops cross our little creek here and disappear into the jungle. The rest of us will open fire as soon as we hear your first machine gun burst." The men all looked at each other and fingered their weapons.

"Yes, I know it's a big gamble. Everything must fall into place with clock-like precision, or we'll take big casualties. I am not much for praying, but if you guys are, now is the time." Phil stood up and walked into the jungle where his corporal had strung up his hammock. "See you in the morning, corporal."

Phil lay in his hammock thinking about how tired he was of seeing only green, how sick he was of the sounds and smells of the jungle. He thought of the nice home he and his wife had built for themselves and their children along California's coastal mountains. He much preferred the sight of the ocean and sounds of pounding surf to the continual jabber of monkeys and squealing of small animals that were being eaten by the other animals higher up on the food chain. It wasn't hard for him to fall asleep.

FOURTEEN

As the major was thinking back over his night's sleep, he could have sworn that he heard a Burmese python slither down the tree above him, stare at him in the dark and then mysteriously disappear. He had immediately gone back to sleep thinking that it was a dream. As he walked around camp carrying his first cup of coffee, he happened to look over into the brush. He gulped as he saw a beautiful but now dead python curled up on the ground near his hammock. Its head had been almost completely cut off with a very sharp knife. He estimated that it was twenty or so feet long. His mouth opened as he contemplated the fate that had awaited him if someone had not quietly dispatched the snake. He might have gotten to his pistol in time, but that would have alerted the Japanese outpost that there was an enemy force in the area. Wow! But who had saved his life and the fate of the mission last night?

He turned and surveyed his men who were in various stages of meal preparation. His gaze stopped on Nang, the Burmese woman who had attached herself to his unit hoping to find some Jap soldiers to kill. She was bent down starting a small fire on which she could cook her rice breakfast. She met his gaze with a big smile, a smile he had not seen since they picked her up several days ago. She said something softly in Burmese that the major did not understand and then went back to preparing her breakfast. She said in a language he did not understand, "Majors need to learn where not to string their hammocks."

Of course, who but a local woman would be aware of the presence of animals in the jungle, and who would be better prepared to kill the dangerous ones? He thought he should thank her, but that would be awkward this morning. So he decided to let it go for now and deal with it later.

She wanted him to thank her, to acknowledge her and let the men know how competent she was with a knife. Not that she was worried about living in the middle of this group of big, burly killers. She just wanted to be one of them, and be the major's favorite if that were possible. As she turned her head back down to fix breakfast, she thought she glimpsed a slight smile on the major's face. She had been a part of this unit long enough to know that that was all she was going to get and should be happy with it.

As Phil finished his breakfast, he was startled by the sounds of rifle and automatic weapons fire coming from the direction of the enemy outpost. He was amazed by how unsynchronized it was, and how little damage it was probably causing. But that is exactly what he had asked for. He crossed is fingers as the private sitting on the ground next to him turned and said, "I didn't know you were superstitious major."

"I am not private; it's bad luck to be superstitious." His men had heard his small attempt at humor many times before. But they knew that they had to laugh or get chewed out later about something totally unconnected. So everyone around him laughed, and the major smiled. He looked at his watch. It was exactly 0600.

The sporadic firing continued for thirty minutes or so and now took on the ferocity of men trained in the art of killing. Then it suddenly stopped and was replaced by the cries of soldiers who were having their throats cut. Then it was quiet. "I think the lieutenant is doing his job," Phil said to no one in particular. Everyone nodded in agreement.

In a few minutes, Lieutenant Schultz and his men came trotting up through the jungle with a bit of pride showing on their faces. "Done as ordered major," the lieutenant said as he sat down in the middle of the group. The major noted that the lieutenant had bloodstains on his hands and some blood running down the front of his shirt.

The lieutenant knew that he was talking about his unit, not the enemy. "No, no one was killed, Private Johnson came away with a small gash on his arm, Sir"

"Good. Get him bandaged up. We are going to need all hands when this fight really gets going. By the way, how is Sergeant Hashimoto doing with that radio?"

"He says he thinks he has the colonel persuaded. I couldn't make out what Sergeant Hashimoto was saying to his radio operator at Jap headquarters, but it sounded convincing to me," the lieutenant said. "He said that the colonel has agreed to send his entire battalion down here in a hurry. He said that he thinks he has fooled them for now, but he wants to stay in touch with the headquarters operator for a little while longer, just in case."

"That sounds like a good idea to me." He turned to the sergeant major sitting next to him. "Sergeant, please pass his report up the line so that everyone is aware of what has happened."

"Yes Sir." The sergeant turned and moved quickly through the underbrush. "Wow. I sure hope this works," he mumbled to himself.

FIFTEEN

I noticed that Phil kept looking at his watch, but that didn't make the time pass more quickly. Every few seconds, he would raise his hand and swat way a mosquito that always came back. Maybe it'll take seven hours, he thought. But seven hours had come and gone. He had posted scouts along the trail who would warn us of the enemy's impending approach, but they were apparently lost in the jungle somewhere. His head dipped against his chest and eyes blinked closed. He had fought sleep all morning, but he was about to lose. The sergeant major was sitting next to him ready to kick him at the first sign of an enemy.

He kept going over his plans in his mind; he could find no flaw in them as long as the entire Japanese battalion marched onto the open trail together. Would he allow all of his troops to be exposed like that if he were in charge? Not likely, he thought. He wondered next if the colonel himself would lead his troops into battle. He knew little about Colonel Maruyama except what he had read in the reports, but he seemed like the kind of leader who would rather stay in his camp and drink scotch. Maybe that would be his undoing the major thought; his thoughts trailed away---

"Hey sergeant, stop kicking me!" His eyes blinked open. The sergeant pointed frantically up the hill to two of their scouts who were standing in a small clearing waving vigorously at them. "Respond sergeant. Let them know we see them and have them get back into formation quickly. Then pass the word down the line that the enemy is at hand."

In about ten minutes, the Japanese soldiers leading the battalion broke out of the jungle along the exposed trail and headed down the mountain toward them. Major Jenkins pulled out his binoculars and stared at the ever- increasing line of Japanese troops. "It looks like the guy in charge is a captain," he said to his sergeant major sitting next to him. "Let's hope that he is not smart enough to see the trap into which he is leading his men."

Everyone in the unit was quiet, peering out over the sights on their weapons and not moving. Keep coming, the major said to himself as the Japanese marched steadily along the trail. Just a few more yards, Phil thought. Then he heard it. From the rear of their column, he heard, and then saw, a courier running down the trail shouting and waving frantically at the Japanese captain. The captain raised his hand to stop the column and wait for the messenger to reach him

The panting courier ran up to the captain, saluted, pulled a piece of paper out of his pocket and handed it to him. "My God, what is going on here?" the sergeant asked quietly. "Where is Sergeant Hashimoto when we need him?" The major responded, "No, they are too far away for us to hear even if we could understand their language." The worried sergeant set his M-1 down. All of the Americans were looking intently at the Japanese column, wondering if they were coming on, or turning around to head back to camp. If we charged down at them now, we could kill two hundred or so, but they would get too many of my boys, the major mused. They are crack troops. What to do? They all stared intently at the column all of which were now getting restless from standing in the hot sun.

The Japanese captain read the message carefully, raised his head and looked directly at Major Jenkins, although he was well camouflaged in the underbrush. Then the captain scanned the hillside where the Americans were trying not to breathe. He folded up the paper, put it inside his shirt pocket and turned to talk to his second in command, a lieutenant. The captain pointed down the trail while talking rapidly to him. The lieutenant nodded, but didn't say anything.

The captain had obviously been presented with a dilemma, and he had to make a decision by himself.

Major Jenkins lowered his head into his cupped hands and could easily visualize his well thought-out plans going down the drain. He remembered that Lieutenant Schultz had said that Sergeant Hashimoto was not sure that the Japanese colonel had completely believed his radio transmission. The colonel must have changed his mind after the column had left the base camp and sent the messenger to order them back before catastrophe struck. But for some reason, the Japanese captain was not totally convinced. He took the message out, read it again, and looked up and down the trail frantically trying to make up his mind.

Then Major Jenkins and all of us heard it, a loud screaming coming up the trail from the direction of the Japanese outpost, which was now in American hands. We all turned to our left and peered out of the underbrush to see what all the commotion was about. What we saw astonished us. A Japanese soldier, apparently wounded, ran limping across the little stream, and up the trail toward the Japanese column. "But wait a minute," the major said. "There are no Japanese troops left at the outpost. Lieutenant Schultz and his band of marauders had killed them all."

The sergeant major said with a steady gaze, "That's no Japanese soldier, major. That's our Sergeant Hashimoto dressed up in an enemy soldier's uniform and running like crazy toward the column."

All of our troops from the major to the lowest private were now watching the clamor with mixed emotions. Should they shoulder their weapons and charge into the Japanese column, killing many, but also suffering casualties of their own? They all looked at their major waiting for orders, but he just stared at the Japanese captain waiting for---he wasn't sure what. Maybe a sign of what he was thinking or what he would do next. Major Jenkins motioned for his men to stay put and to keep quiet above all. Their discipline kept them down and unseen by the enemy. One sudden move or burst of noise could be their end, but they were well trained, and their training won the day.

"What the hell is he doing?" asked the sergeant major. The disguised Japanese-American frantically motioned the Japanese soldiers to follow him back toward the outpost screaming, running back and forth to try to get them moving. Ignoring the waving and stammering of their senior officer and persuaded by the prospect of wiping out an entire American battalion, the Japanese soldiers grabbed their weapons, and shoved their captain out of the way as they rushed to follow Sergeant Hashimoto. Their captain threw his hands in the air and turned to follow his troops now headed into a certain ambush. Their discipline collapsed!

"Damn major. The sarge has them eating out of his hands!"

"He is no longer Sergeant Hashimoto. He is now Lieutenant Hashimoto," declared the major with relief. They turned back and pointed their weapons toward the column, each throwing a round into the chamber as quietly as the weapons allowed.

SIXTEEN

As I recall, the battle didn't take very long. In fact, it was not much of a battle at all. Our six machine guns opened up on the enemy almost in unison, scattering the Japanese soldiers in all directions. They didn't know where to aim their weapons because the firing came from inside a dense jungle across the creek. Some of their soldiers dove down into the streambed hoping that we would think they were dead. But they hadn't counted on Nang! The diminutive villager's revenge proved swift and sure.

The firing stopped, and I saw Phil stand up to survey the area. "We need to make sure that they are all dead, sergeant, before we leave here." This was the part of a battle that he hated the most, and he usually delegated it to someone else. "I guess the colonel was not with them."

"Hey, where is my bowie knife?" I yelled. Everyone looked at me to see what the fuss was all about. I lifted up my empty scabbard to show everyone that I was not crazy.

"Look down in the streambed," a private said pointing.

There she was, sweet little Nang, the modest and tiny Burmese woman wielding my knife like it was a hatchet. No one was spared. She didn't care if the Jap soldier was dead or alive; she was going to finish him off with a quick slice of my razor sharp blade. Occasionally, she would come upon a wounded soldier who pleaded for his life, but to no avail. Swish! She had no mercy and was glad to find one alive so that she could finish what the Americans had started.

The men set their weapons down and began taking bets on how many live ones were still left. They cheered her on as she would rise up and wave her hand with a big yell when she found one she could kill. She finally reached the end of the line of soldiers who had tried to escape along the streambed. She then climbed up onto the trail itself and worked her way back toward the American troops, one wounded Jap at a time.

We all reached for our weapons when she came across a Japanese sergeant who apparently had been playing dead. He jumped up, pulled out his knife and lunged at her. But before anyone could cock his rifle and finish him off, Nang blocked the lunge and swung her knife at him. Neither scored; they were locked in mortal combat. The soldiers couldn't fire for fear of hitting her, so they put their rifles down and watched in amazement. With both hands locked up with her adversary, she pulled him in close, near enough to smell his breath, and then brought her right knee up and connected a solid blow to his groin.

The men all groaned and grabbed their crotches knowing how that must have hurt; they looked back in time to see her run her knife into his back as he lay bent over in pain. She finally made it back to the assembled soldiers, smiled, wiped off the knife and gave it back to me. I put the knife into its scabbard, turned it around and handed it back to her. "Nang, you wielded this knife like I never could. Here, it's yours." The men all cheered. Nang took it with a big smile. She strapped it under her sash and wondered if her murdered sisters were looking down from heaven with approval. I later learned to regret that act of generosity, but that's getting ahead of my story.

SEVENTEEN

We had marched several hours along the trail that now rose abruptly into the mountains. There was no doubt now that we were headed in the right direction, toward the Japanese headquarters camp located on top of the mountain ahead. Near sunset, we were still a couple of hours away. We came across a clearing in the forest on which our troops could set up camp for the night. As we rose higher in altitude, the jungle gradually opened up giving way to scattered trees and heavy brush. The air thinned out too as we climbed the mountain; it was much cooler and easier to breathe. No wonder the colonel selected this location for his headquarters, Major Jenkins thought. No one would ever think of looking up here for him. We will rest tonight and surprise him in the morning. The major sat on a log staring into a small fire the corporal had built for him. He was sipping his coffee lost in thought about the next day when he looked up to see Nang and their Burmese scout, whose name he still couldn't remember, walking toward him. The scout said to him, "Sir, is it okay if we talk to you a minute? Nang here has something she wants to say to you. I will translate her words directly, as if she were speaking."

After the grim work she performed on the enemy today, the major was not about to deny her whatever she wanted. "Sure. Sit down you two, and let's have a chat." He was happy for the diversion.

"Major, there are some things that I don't understand about your army. Although I let my friend here speak for me, I have learned enough English to understand much of what you all say to each other. Remember, the English occupied us before the war started. In fact, many of my people were happy to see the Japanese invade Burma and run the despised English out of our country. Most of us learned what a mistake that was with regret.

"I have watched the Japanese forces come and go through this jungle for the past four years and have been struck by how cruel the officers are to their men. They will beat them for very little reason, sometimes, I think, just to prove that the officers are in charge. A soldier will often get beaten for making a judgment on his own, because he went beyond what his officer had ordered him to do. I would imagine that this could be a problem in battle, because situations come up for which the officers have not planned, and the enlisted men cannot respond without orders from above. Their military system seems to have built-in flaws.

"On the other hand, as I watch you lead your men, in a way that seems to go down to your senior sergeants; also, I notice a different approach to leadership. First of all, you are very polite to them. More importantly, you accept, and even request, their opinions and suggestions. Everyone seems to be a part of the decision making process in your army." Phil smiled, thinking of some of the cruel sergeants with whom he had served in basic training, but he let her continue.

"So, my question is, is your leadership style based on your system of political freedom, or is it in your culture? To you Americans, this whole issue may be no big deal, but it is very curious to those of us who live in different countries."

Phil stared down at the ground using his stick to draw figures in the dust as he thought of an answer. "Yes, your observation is basically accurate but not always so. We have some officers who would just as soon beat their men, but the army doesn't allow that. I think there is an inherent difference that may be culturally based, but more likely reality based.

"No, that's not exactly true either. All armies have the same problem; members of the leadership corps are often the ones who are targeted first by their enemy for destruction in battle. We always try to locate and aim at the enemy officers first, because we know that the loss of their leader will cause confusion in their ranks until another officer can be found.

"At West Point, our military academy, we read the story of a Civil War battle in which the Union Army took out the Confederate's commanding officer by long range sniper fire just seconds before their attack began. His death caused such confusion in his army that the Confederate battalion was overwhelmed before it could get organized to respond.

"The same thing happened in the battle of Savo Island off Guadalcanal in the summer of 1942. The Allied fleet commander, a British or Australian admiral as I recall, failed to designate a second in command and did not notify the captains of his ships that he was going ashore to meet with our marine general. Superior Japanese naval forces attacked his fleet while he was gone, and four of our heavy cruisers were sunk while their captains were waiting for orders that never came. We cannot let that happen to us.

"You may not be aware, but our entire unit here is organized in line-of-command order. In other words, no two men, even if they are the same rank, are equal in seniority or authority. For example, every corporal knows who the senior corporal is and so on down the line. If I am taken out, Captain Beltrans immediately takes over, no questions asked. And Lieutenant Schultz takes command if both Captain Beltrans and I are killed, again, with no questions asked. This chain of command goes all the way down to the lowest private. Our unit will never be defeated because no one knew who was in command.

"This means that every man in our unit has the potential to be in command. One of the main jobs of a commander is to train his men to be ready to plan and make decisions in battle. The best way to do this is to let them offer suggestions and ideas, encourage them to make decisions and, above all, not criticize or punish them when they do. Consequently, when ideas are offered, I will often take them in place of my own. Remember, a person will always work harder to be sure that his idea works than he would to support someone else's plan. That's just human nature, some would call it machismo." He couldn't help but smile.

"However, there is another issue here. My dad would often tell me on the farm that no one knows how to do a job better than the man doing it. On the farm, that could be important. On the battlefield, it could be critical. Consequently, I listen to what the privates say as often as I listen to what the generals say. Our lives often depend upon it."

The soldiers within hearing distance all pretended that they were not listening, but if the major had been watching, he would have seen a smile on everyone's bearded face.

"You will remember what happened today to the Japanese unit when they were confronted with the orders from their colonel to return to base rather than continue on to rescue fellow soldiers under attack. Their captain had orders and reason to believe that they were headed into an ambush. Rather than talk it over with his men and give them the evidence he received that there was an enemy force waiting to wipe them out, he acted entirely on his own. The soldiers knew that their captain would pay no attention to their opinion, so they took matters into their own hands and rushed past their commander into a deadly ambush.

"If we had been in the same circumstances, I would have shared my information with my unit, asked what they thought and then convinced them that it would be suicide to march on. Today's battle showed the big difference between the Japanese and American armies, and it cost them almost three hundred men, and illustrated why we are going to win this war. Fanatic individuals don't win wars. Men dedicated to working with each other do.

"For example, look at the actions Lieutenant Hashimoto took today that turned the tide of battle and insured our victory. I did not order him to do what he did; in fact we never even discussed the possibility. He saw, from his vantage point at the bottom end of the trail, that something was wrong. He remembered that in his conversation with the Japanese radio operator, he had said something that led the operator to realize that he was not talking to one of his own soldiers. The colonel was alerted, and the messenger was sent to retrieve the column before it was too late. The messenger arrived in time, but their culture of command, if I may use that phrase, came into play, and they were all killed, thanks to our lieutenant's swift and critical action.

"So you can see how important that cultural leadership can be. The Japanese soldier is the bravest and most dedicated combatant I have ever seen, or could ever imagine. But that skill does not necessarily translate into victory. It won battles three hundred years ago, but that samurai spirit does not win wars in the twentieth century. Their failure to recognize that reality will bring about their ultimate defeat."

It had been quiet for a while; when Phil yawned. Everyone in his command knew that when the major yawned, the conversation was over. Even Nang seemed to get the point. "Maybe we can continue our conversation at some later time major," she said standing up with a smile. "I would like that," he replied walking over to his hammock and crawling in.

There is is more to this woman than what we see, more than she lets on, Phil thought as he dozed off. She has a higher intelligence than the average illiterate village girl. I've got to check this out. He began to snore.

EIGHTEEN

The Japanese camp was well situated on the cleared summit of the tallest mountain in the region. As we crawled up to it, I saw the rising sun flag fluttering from a tall pole in the middle of what the U.S. Army would call the parade grounds. The colonel's office at the far end, was made out of bamboo and obviously designed with the comfort of the commander in mind. It had a porch with a sentry standing guard under the overhang and two rooms inside. In the first room sat the colonel's secretary, a young corporal. He did the typing, issued the colonel's orders, made his tea and did what the colonel ordered. It was a whole lot better than carrying a rifle and battling enemy soldiers. The colonel sat in the back office with a slow-turning ceiling fan keeping him cool, just like one would see in the south sea movies Hollywood made in the 30's. The rain had stopped, and the humidity was on the rise as the sun broke through the rapidly moving clouds. The soldiers on both sides were tired of the monsoons, but the rainy season was not due to end for a few more weeks. The colonel heard a knock on his door and bid his typist to enter. The corporal came in, bowed and handed the colonel papers to sign. He then turned and walked out closing the door behind him. As he turned to move toward his desk, he suddenly felt a hand clamp over his mouth from behind. Then he felt the blade of a razor sharp army knife slide quietly but firmly across his throat. The hand stayed in place until the corporal was no longer conscious. The assassin helped the corporal slide without sound to the floor. That was all the corporal was to know in this life. The guard at the front door was next. Neither death made a sound. Our men were good at their trade.

The colonel heard a soft knock at his door. What does the corporal want this time? He thought as he was reading the reports he was to sign. The door opened, but the colonel did not look up. "Yes corporal, what do you want?" There was no response. The colonel looked up to see who was interrupting his work. He found himself staring into the business end of a Thompson sub-machine gun being held by a serious looking American major with a many-weeks-old scraggly beard. The colonel jumped out of his chair. "Who are you? What do you want?" he asked in English. He automatically reached for his sword at his belt and then thought better of it.

Phil did not respond at first. He just stared back at the colonel. Three more American soldiers and I squeezed into his office all carrying various weapons. "Please sit down Colonel Maruyama, but first, I would like you to remove your samurai sword. I want to show my grandkids that I really was in World War II." The colonel reluctantly

"I don't know who you are, but I must remind you that my battalion is returning to camp as we speak, and when they arrive, you will be----." He didn't say the word, but ran his hand across his throat in an obvious gesture. Phil pulled up the one chair in the room and bid his men to make themselves as comfortable as possible. Obviously, the colonel did not want to talk to more than one person at a time in his office.

"Oh yes, your battalion." Phil turned slightly. "Sergeant major, would you please return his battalion's flag to the colonel here?" The sergeant pulled a battered and bloody flag out of his shirt and tossed it onto the colonel's desk. "Sorry for its condition colonel, but battles can be bloody." The room was quiet as the colonel stared down at his beloved battalion flag, one that he had designed himself. "You must have taken serious casualties to kill this many Japanese troops, major," the colonel said calmly when he finally regained his composure.

"Actually, we had only one man injured with a cut in his arm." The room was quiet again as the colonel, sweat now showing on his brow, tried to comprehend the magnitude of what Major Jenkins was saying. "I would try to explain to you how we accomplished this, but it would take too much of your valuable time. "By the way colonel, let me introduce myself. I am Major Phillip Jenkins, and this is my special unit of the 5307th, better known as Merrill's Marauders. My exec, Captain Ray Beltrans is the tough looking Indian sitting over in the

"You and I first met at Myitkyina; you may recall that my men struck your left flank in a classic surprise attack that routed your almost victorious forces. You should have taken precautions to protect your left flank you know. Unfortunately, we were unable to prevent your escape." The colonel scowled and nodded in acknowledgement.

We now began to hear the sounds of men being killed in the parade grounds and in their barracks. Screams and muffled shots rang out as the few Japanese soldiers remaining in camp were individually eliminated. "Sorry for the racket colonel, but war can be noisy as well as bloody." Then the noise stopped. The colonel tried to imagine how his troops had been caught off guard. "Don't feel bad. You will be joining them soon, but your death will be by hanging, not by rifle or knife. It is not nearly as noisy, and we are running short of ammunition." His men looked at each other.

The colonel gathered his composure, "What puzzles me major is why your army is so dedicated to my capture and execution? You and your men have walked over a thousand miles to get to Burma and then over five hundred miles to get to us here in the mountains and all without being detected. On the way, you whipped us at Myitkyina. These are indeed great accomplishments, and I compliment you for them. But why are you so obsessed with me?"

The major exhaled, put his feet up on the colonel's desk, leaned back in his bamboo chair, lit the cigar he was saving for this occasion and thought before responding. "I

"Ah yes. Now I see," the colonel responded. "Our 'uncivilized' behavior against an occupied country somehow struck a chord in your Army's soul that demanded revenge. Could this be an example of punishing someone for doing the same thing that you have done, some feeling of guilt over the behavior of your own culture? We must eradicate the 'evil' Japanese before they do the same thing America has done to its native inhabitants since the early seventeenth century?" He looked at me questionably. "Oh, and let's not forget the Negroes in your midst. How many of them have you Americans lynched lately? And how many of them do you have in your 'Integrated' unit?"

The major took a long drag on his cigar and squinted at the colonel. "Oh yes, now I get a lecture on the behavior of the American settlers who brutally wiped out thousands of Indian inhabitants of North America. And of course how we still treat the Negroes in our midst. Yes, I am familiar with our history colonel and fail to see its relevance to your murder of innocent Burmese civilians today. By the way, I am impressed with your ability to speak English."

"You Americans are the most linguistically illiterate people in the world. You barely know one language and are amazed at those of us who know several. I was a member of the Japanese military legation in Washington when Admiral Yamamoto was our naval attaché in the 1920's. By the way, his death sealed our fate when your P-38's shot his plane down in April of 1943 over Bougainville in the Solomons. His death was such a pity. He was the only leader we had who might have won this war for us." The colonel folded his hands looking satisfied.

"So your stint in Washington is why you know so much about our history, colonel?" Phil responded while blowing his cigar smoke toward the ceiling fan.

"Only partially." The colonel sat up in his chair. "We studied world history at our military academy when I was in training. It fascinated me. What particularly interested me was the frequency with which armies have massacred innocent civilians during the many wars that humanity has fought over the past two thousand years."

"You are not trying to tell me that your behavior here in Burma can be justified by comparing it to historical events," the major asked.

"Well of course. Where do you think we Japanese learned it? We didn't invent brutality. But don't agree with me just because I say so."

"Don't worry, I won't," Phil looked at his men with what they knew was an expression of restrained boredom. "Look at the record," the colonel continued, "And where did it start? Let's first review the Punic Wars in, what was it, second and third century BC I believe. The Carthaginians and the Romans battled each other for control of ocean commerce in the Mediterranean. International trade was at stake, and so this conflict went back and forth for years with no winner. In spite of what your Admiral Mahan said, control of the sea did not result in control of their world. For over one hundred years, the Phoenician and Roman empires fought each other, killing hundreds of thousands of each others' soldiers and sailors. Then the Romans figured out that they could only conquer their archenemy by invading their homeland and wiping them out, man, woman and child. Then Roman troops landed in North Africa and invaded their enemy's capital, Carthage, massacring the entire population. Without civilian support, the Carthaginian soldiers could no longer fight, and the war soon ended in Rome's favor. For the past two thousand years, there has been no one living in what was once the largest city along the Mediterranean. Today, it is inhabited only by Berber tribesmen and their sheep. So the question is, was it better to slaughter all of their civilians and end the war, or to kill thousands of additional troops in a continuing stalemate?"

The major stared at the colonel through the maze of cigar smoke now hanging over his desk.

Corporal Robertson had been wandering around the colonel's office opening doors and checking storage racks. "Look what I found here major, a bottle of ten- year-old scotch whiskey and two glasses. Would you like me to pour you a shot?"

"Yes corporal and thank you. And one for the colonel too please." The colonel winced visibly at the major's politeness to an enlisted man. "Remember what Winston Churchill once said, 'When you are about to kill a man, it doesn't hurt to be polite to him.' Phil liked that quotation, but hadn't been able to use it recently.

"You are very kind, major, to offer me a glass of my own whiskey. I have saved it for special occasions, and this seems to be one." We four thirsty men sitting on the floor licked our lips, but Major Jenkins pretended not to notice.

"My this is good," the colonel said looking over at the bottle now sitting on his desk. "The Scots really know how to make whiskey." Looking up at the major, he continued, "I think this comes from the part of the world in which your ancestors lived. Is that not true?" as he downed a second swallow. "Let me think, I believe that Jenkins is a Scottish name is it not?"

"You are close Colonel. My ancestors actually came from Wales, which, as you probably know, is very near Scotland. Both have a Celtic heritage. Most last names that end in an 's' are Welch."

"Hmm, oh yes, and you were overwhelmed by the English King Edward in, what was it the twelfth or thirteenth century? You ancestors fought very bravely and held out for years against a much larger army. But it was interesting that after being defeated, your soldiers changed sides and joined King Edward in his fight against your neighbors, the Scots. I wonder why that was. Maybe they were trying to learn how to make whiskey." No one but the colonel smiled at his little joke. Colonel Maruyama was enjoying his history review. But he could see that he wasn't getting far with it.

Major Jenkins scowled. "Your point eludes me."

"Ah, well said major. I must remember that reply for future use." The irony of that remark didn't pass unnoticed by the men in the colonel's bamboo office that hot and humid morning

NINETEEN

Major Jenkins issued a few routine orders to his sergeant major, mostly about loading up the enemy's food onto their mules and getting the men packed up and ready to return to their home base five hundred miles away. "It's going to be a long march colonel, as I am sure you are aware."

"Yes, I know. You don't mind if I have another scotch, do you?"

"Please, help yourself, but I interrupted your history lesson justifying why it is okay to kill civilians in wartime," Phil said with enough sarcasm to make his point. He was not aware that some of his troops, including Nang, were sitting outside the office listening to the exchange.

"It's not exactly a justification major, but I guess it is a history lesson. You Americans are not only devoid of foreign language skills; you are even more remiss in studying history. I think the next lesson that we learned came from the Crusades that your Christian Church waged on the people of the Middle East a thousand years ago. The point of the Crusades was to capture Jerusalem from the infidel and return it to Christian hands. Unfortunately for the locals, the Christian Army decided to practice killing on the civilian Greeks living in Constantinople and Asia Minor before they arrived at the Holy Land. We will never know how many hundreds of thousands of innocent civilians were butchered along the way. Of course there was no reason for this massacre except to terrify the armies up ahead; it didn't work however. The Muslim Armies were not impressed.

"Probably the most classic example of civilian terror was the invasion by the Mongols into Europe in the thirteenth century. Their tactic was simple. They would invade a town, massacre its population and let one person escape and ride to the next town to spread the word. The towns soon became so terrified of the Mongols that they surrendered without a fight when they heard they were coming. What could be more effective in war than that?

"But the one I love the most is your Civil War. Neither side could achieve victory until General Sherman came along and wisely said, 'War is hell.' He wasn't philosophizing; he was telling the Confederates what they could expect from him, and he delivered. His march through Georgia and the two Carolinas is classic, brutal warfare. He burned towns, demolished railroads, destroyed crops and laid waste to the civilian population of the south. The Union victory was assured after that.

"World War I was an example of how not to win a war. As you probably know, in the fall of 1918, the Allies, with the help of American reinforcements, drove the German army back through Belgium and into Germany. The Kaiser wisely sued for peace, surrendering his massive but as yet undefeated army. History and the German people have always wondered why he did that. What history fails to acknowledge is that the English naval blockade of Europe had starved the civilian population of both Germany and its ally, Austria. The Kaiser knew that his army could not win if its civilian backbone was starved to death; so he gave up to protect them. Unfortunately, the fact that the German civilians had not been attacked and decimated turned their bitterness of defeat into World War II which is a very good example of my point."

"Yes, but you haven't heard the best yet. Now we get to World War II and my country's attack on Pearl Harbor, the most unfortunate and ill-advised attack ever perpetuated on a potential enemy."

"Wait a minute. Are you saying that the Japanese attack on Pearl Harbor was a mistake?" The major set his glass of scotch on the desk. "Tell me about it."

"Of course it was a mistake! What did it accomplish? The eight battleships we sunk or damaged were ancient, and they were sunk in forty or so feet of water. Since their draft was typically over thirty feet, all but one was easily refloated in the shallow water and repaired within two years. None of America's aircraft carriers were even in Pearl Harbor at the time of attack, so what, tactically, was achieved? We awoke the sleeping giant and sealed our defeat. How short-sighted was that?"

"Now I am interested colonel. How would you have planned and carried out the Pearl Harbor raid?"

"Actually, I did make a proposal that would have insured our victory, but no one at Tokyo headquarters would listen to me. Hence I was stationed here in Burma where I couldn't embarrass anyone. My plan was based on the fact that an adversary has only one chance to make a surprise attack on its enemy, and therefore, it must be a good one. Ours was half-hearted. Think what damage our six aircraft carriers and three hundred-fifty planes could have done if they had sailed on from Pearl Harbor and also attacked San Francisco.

"Since we were already at Pearl Harbor on December 7th, we should have sent our planes back for a second strike to take out the fuel storage tanks and the dry dock facilities in the harbor. There was no excuse for not doing so. Admiral Yamamoto had selected Admiral Nagumo as the fleet commander because he was the most senior

"What would the U.S. fleet have done if all of its fuel had been destroyed at Pearl Harbor? That was all the oil you had or could get for at least a year. And how would you have repaired your sunken battleships without the drydocks? Admiral Nagumo headed back for Japan after sinking eight old battleships and accomplishing nothing. I would rather not think about how close we came to a complete victory. Shortsighted and incompetent leaders doomed us.

"The next attack should have been made on San Francisco to destroy the major military bases in the Bay Area. After decimating your fleet at Pearl Harbor, we could have sailed on to the coast of California without opposition or fear. In five days, our fleet could have been sitting off San Francisco launching planes and attacking unopposed. Your Air Corps had no fighter planes within a thousand miles. Let's identify the bases that we could have destroyed,

"Since we would have had no opposition, our planes could also have returned again and again to bomb and strafe the civilian population of the Bay Area. Then Americans would have known what General Sherman meant by 'War is Hell.'

"Just think of how quickly the war would have ended with a U.S. surrender if all of those facilities had been destroyed and thousands of civilians had been killed a week after Pearl Harbor! The San Francisco area would have been a charred wasteland. We could have landed troops unopposed in both Canada and Mexico, marched south and north into your country and forced surrender terms on you from which you would have never recovered!

"As Admiral Yamamoto was reported to have said, 'We will negotiate your surrender on the steps of the Capitol.' That was a dream that could have come true if our General Staff had only listened to me. Instead, we will be subjected to a humiliating and disastrous defeat, all because we attacked Pearl Harbor half-heartedly and left mainland United States untouched."

The colonel was very satisfied with his history lesson and sat back in his chair. "So what are we doing here in Burma, thousands of miles from the important fighting you ask?" The major didn't know he had asked. "We had great plans to march through Burma and into India and link up with Hitler's forces coming down from Egypt somewhere in the Middle East. Unfortunately, General Rommel became bogged down in the desert sands of North Africa and never made it to the Suez Canal as planned. But we got close. Remember when our fleet sailed unopposed into the Indian Ocean in early 1942, all the way to Madagascar. And where were our allies? They were still battling the British Army in Egypt, so our fleet had to turn around and go home. What a waste of a grand plan, a plan that would have given us the whole world.

"Burma was our linkage to India and beyond, but we were defeated in our attempt to conquer India, even though many Indian leaders were rooting and fighting for us against the British. We even built railroads through this pitiful jungle with prisoner labor to facilitate the supply of our victorious troops. We were pushed back here where we have spent the war without hope of being a contributor to its outcome. Do you ever stop and think major that whatever we do here will have absolutely no effect on the outcome of the war? Scary isn't it?"

The colonel continued. "My commanding general in Rangoon, General Hyotaro, has not communicated with me for months. He probably has forgotten that we are up here. We must live off the land and end up killing civilians and steal their food just to survive. We are not unlike your General Sherman and his troops when the world lost track of them as they marched through Georgia."

The major must have thought that the colonel was beginning to make sense, even though he would never admit it. Phil could visualize the death and havoc the Japanese carrier force would have rained down on his beloved California if their high command had followed the colonel's plan. We dodged a bullet, he thought.

The colonel stared out of the window into the forest dreaming of what might have been. He soon pulled himself back and turned to the major.

"In summary major, no war will ever be won until the civilian population is treated the same way we treat enemy soldiers. Look at Nanking in China. How terrified the Chinese were when they heard of our treatment of their women and children! Countries will surrender only when they fear that the enemy will get to their families if they do not sue for peace. We have instilled fear and anger in the people here in Burma by massacring villagers. Consequently, their Army is afraid of us, so you have come all this way to kill us."

"So what does the future hold? Do you think that this will be civilization's last war?" the major asked puffing his cigar.

"I don't think so," the colonel responded pensively. "Will future wars be initiated by leaders who have studied history and know what it takes to win? I doubt it. It hasn't happened yet. Does that make villains out of us who do know how to win? According to you

Americans it does. And since you will be the winners of this war, you get to write its history.

"All I ask major is that you treat us with honesty. We are a small country and had no other way to win accept by acting with cruelty toward our enemies in hopes of terrifying them into surrender. We failed to apply terror when we should have on your West Coast, and we over- applied it in Asia when it only riled up you Americans.

"My request Major, is please don't let your country start future wars unless you are willing to accept cruelty as a natural part of them. Don't kid yourself into thinking that there is a moral war, a successful one without cruelty toward civilians. It has never happened, and it never will. The history that you write will downplay your own actions in this war, but we both know that you could not have won without it. The big example of this of course, is the firebombing of Tokyo and the total destruction of Hiroshima and Nagasaki a few days ago. How many innocent civilians were killed in just those three attacks, maybe a half million? We will probably never know, will we? But Japan would never surrender if you had not massacred hundreds of thousands of our civilians in those attacks.

"You see major, you Americans have made war too easy. When war gets easy, countries will conduct more of it, more often, for less and less justification. You have invented weapons that fight battles without using soldiers in wars that civilians don't even know or care are being fought.

"Armies will be professional and all volunteer and won't need to be supplemented by draftees. If a war gets bigger, you will hire mercenaries to do the job for you rather than induct reluctant young men into the service. Remember the riots in New York City during your Civil War when President Lincoln tried to initiate a draft? Mercenaries have been around for thousands of years, so maybe the next war will be fought using only mercenaries or maybe using some kind of mechanical soldiers. Wow! That would be something wouldn't it?

"Wars will end only when the civilian population feels the suffering of the soldiers on the battlefield, as General Sherman said.

However, aggressive countries will do everything they can to keep their people from experiencing the horrors of war. Someday, countries will get so manipulative that they will even lower taxes during the conflict to keep the home folks happy. Wars will never end as long as the population can be kept unaware of its consequences."

Phil opened his mouth, but nothing came out.

The colonel calmed down a little, seeing that he probably wasn't getting through to Major Jenkins. "Again, all I ask of you in exchange for my life is honesty. Can you do that major?" The colonel poured himself his last scotch. He held the empty bottle up and looked at it. "The epitome of man's creative genius," he said as he savored the last drop.

"You ask a great deal, colonel, probably more than I can deliver. However, your life is not a bargaining chip. We have not marched fifteen hundred miles to listen to your history lesson and then let you return home. Sergeant, is the execution tree ready?"

"Yes sir."

"Good, let's get this thing over with." "You mean my murder, major."

"Yes. I don't like killing people, even mortal enemies, so I normally leave it to others who are more comfortable with it. But this one is mine," he concluded with a smile.

TWENTY

Two soldiers walked over to the colonel and, each taking an arm, lifted him up and walked him to the door. They stepped out of the bamboo office into the bright sunlight now filling the parade grounds. As his eyes became accustomed to the glare, the colonel could see a rope dangling from a tree branch at the other end of the clearing, ending in a hangman's noose about six feet off the ground. He stopped to look around for the last time. He saw his six remaining battalion officers tied up, each to his own tree, with a look of terror in their eyes.

Someone had brought out a chair and set it under the noose. The major pick up the colonel's beautiful sword from his desk and admired it. Putting it in its case and then the case under his arm, he followed the group onto the parade grounds.

The colonel looked to his right at the edge of the clearing and the trees that surrounded it. He spotted Nang standing behind a much larger corporal, but she was not completely out of sight. He stopped suddenly, and his mouth dropped open. He jerked around toward Major Jenkins who was following the procession. "Major. Do you know who that Burmese woman standing over there is?" He pointed with his chin since his hands were tied behind his back.

"Sure do colonel. Her name is Nang, and she attached herself to our unit several days ago after your men massacred everyone living in her village, including her parents and sisters. I must say, she has learned to kill Japanese soldiers very well."

The colonel burst out laughing. "So, she has taken you in too. Her name may be Nang, but she is not some simple village girl who has innocently attached herself to you and is learning how to kill Japanese soldiers. She is a seasoned Burmese terrorist who has temporarily joined forces with you Americans to help rid her country of all foreigners. She is an experienced killer who is notorious in this jungle for stalking and killing our soldiers in their sleep. She moves through the jungle like a cat, and I would guess that you are alive today only because she has some use for you.

"She hates the English as much as the Japanese and will do whatever is necessary to rid her country of all foreigners when the war ends. I hope you can make it out of Burma before she turns on you. And by the way, she speaks very fluent English, so be careful what you say around her."

The major looked around, but Nang had successfully hidden herself behind the big corporal. Phil stroked his beard and thought of Rudyard Kipling's poem, "The female of the species is more deadly than the male." He would deal with that later. He had other fish to fry now.

The procession again started moving quietly toward the hanging tree. When they reached the chair, the two soldiers lifted the colonel up onto it in a standing position and slipped the noose around his neck. A private came running up to the major and whispered something into his ear. The major nodded and turned back to the colonel now standing in the office chair with his hands tied behind his back and the noose snug around his neck.

"Well colonel, I guess the time has come. We have been enemies for four years, you and I. We almost met at Myitkyina, but you out maneuvered me then and made us track you up here into this godforsaken wilderness. My men have never given up, and it has finally paid off." He liked to give his men credit, even though he deserved most of it himself. "This is the day we have worked for."

His men were obviously tired of listening to the major's speeches, but maybe one more would be okay. They all began to strap their large packs on their backs and pick up their weapons. They turned for the last time to watch the execution. The major noticed that Nang had worked her way around the group and had ended up standing next to the six remaining Japanese officers who were tied up and sitting on the ground. She had pulled out her newly acquired bowie knife, and her fingers caressed its sharp edge. She had a smile on her face.

"In our next lives colonel, let's return as friends and drink our scotch together at the Imperial Hotel bar in Tokyo while sharing war stories and describing the women we have loved."

"I would like that major," as he smiled down from his chair. "And by the way. Take good care of that sword. It is priceless."

The major turned away from the colonel, looked down at his newly acquired possession, and then turned back. "By the way colonel, I forgot to tell you, our radio just picked up a dispatch relayed to us from Tokyo. It said that your emperor has just agreed to all allied surrender terms. Japan has given up. The war is over!"

Before he could see the expression on the colonel's face, Phil reached out with his right foot and kicked the chair out from under him. His men gasped and looked away from their dying enemy now swinging by his neck in the breeze.

With their Burmese scout in the lead and in single file, they began their long march down the trail and back to civilization. The major swung his pack onto his back and reached for his tommy gun.

"Major. Aren't you taking us with you?" the Japanese captain sitting on the ground pleaded. The major stroked his beard. He was getting proud of his new growth of hair. "I think not captain. It's best if you wait here. The local Burmese civilians who live down the hill will come up and release you," he said as he smiled, "and Nang here will protect you from jungle animals until they arrive."

"Major, please. You can't do that. She will torture us slowly one at a time with that knife of hers until we all die a horrible, painful death."

Major Jenkins slipped his weapon over his shoulder, stowed the colonel's sword in his belt, and began walking down the trail. He looked back over his shoulder, "You may be right captain. But remember, war is hell!"

TWENTY-ONE

The rain continued to fall, sometimes in sprinkles, sometimes in torrents. Occasionally, the clouds would break and the sun would pop out and then disappear again behind a swarm of black clouds streaming up from the Indian Ocean. The men wore their rain slickers and broad brimmed Australian hats to protect them from most of the rain as they sloshed through the mud and water with the singular determination of soldiers going home.

One could see that they were all happy that the war was over. They had survived, an extraordinary feat in itself in this part of the world, but they weren't home yet. Still, the major had reminded them to "Keep your powder dry," as soldiers had been told since gunpowder was invented, "and keep your weapons within reach. Yes, the war is over, but we are a combat unit in unfamiliar territory, very close to the Chinese border; we might need to defend ourselves against an unknown enemy from any direction at any moment."

"Yea, against who?" I heard Private Skapinski remark.

Grumbling is standard procedure in armies around the world and across centuries, and the constant rain didn't help or make the walk home any easier. The major calculated that the Monsoon would end in a week or so, but not today. "More is the pity," he remembered his father saying when he was a little boy. He could never quite figure out what his father meant by that.

It was the second day since we had left the Japanese camp on the hill, the colonel swinging in the wind and the six Japanese officers pleading for their lives. We were all glad to be out of earshot of those poor bastards screaming and crying for help. No telling what Nang did to them or how slowly they died, and we didn't want to know. Did Phil have a problem with leaving their execution in the hands of a woman bent on revenge? "No, I did not, in spite of the colonel's argument, or maybe because of it," the major said to me.

"But we were only following orders," the Japanese officers pleaded.

"How many times have I heard that excuse from Japanese prisoners?"

As Major Jenkins reviewed Colonel Maruyama's arguments, he knew that they were wrong, but he needed to formulate his own response that made military and moral sense. He told himself that morality trumps military needs, or at least that's what he has always thought. Now he must frame that argument in his own mind, or it would haunt him forever. He had never killed civilians, at least none of which he was aware.

The main argument as he often expressed it to me is that civilians, by their very nature, are unarmed and unable to protect themselves or fight back. "There! That's all that needs to be said. The same reason you don't pick on someone smaller than you or attack an enemy without declaring war first. This needs more thought," as if he were not totally convinced of the logic of his argument. The colonel's words haunted him.

Going downhill was hardest when it rained. The mud destroyed any possibility of having a sound footing. With heavy packs on their backs, the men slipped and slid along the descending trail, some falling into a piles of backpacks and M-1 rifles. It often took two or three other soldiers to get the victim upright and moving again. The major could hear swearing coming from the men in front of the column. Swearing was good, he thought. It meant that they were glad to be headed home.

"Keeping these mules from falling to their deaths and taking our supplies with them is getting to be a real problem, major." His sergeant major was always close by with his latest worry.

"Yes, sergeant, thank you for your observation," Phil replied. He hated it when people brought up the obvious. He glanced down from the trail to the roaring creek at the bottom of the canyon below them. He hated heights almost as much as he hated snakes. He turned and quietly looked back up the trail. He worked hard trying to keep his spirits up as the rain kept coming down. Unfortunately, the mule carrying our radio had fallen to the bottom of the canyon killing the mule and destroying the radio. We were now out of contact with our main base and were on our own.

Where is Nang? We wondered. She had not rejoined the unit, after they left her yesterday to deal with the Japanese officers. Occasionally, he would turn and look back to see if she were following them. "I have lots of questions to ask her," he muttered to me.

As we dropped lower in altitude, the jungle began to creep around us again. I don't know if the temperature or the humidity was worse, he thought as their progress slowed. Each step in the mud was more difficult; just pulling a foot up and out of the muck and then replacing it ahead was a trial. There was no sun to be seen, but his wristwatch told the major that it was getting close to stopping time. "Is Captain Beltrans finding us a place to spend the night?" he shouted at me. I waved and nodded from the lead.

The rain was lightening up just a little now, raising everyone's spirits as we pulled off the trail into an open spot. I was standing in the middle of a clearing and yelled back at the major, "Is this spot okay major?"

It was at nighttime that Phil's conscience bothered him the most. The men typically left him alone after dinner with his own thoughts, which seemed to haunt him more each night. I, as the executive officer, was the only one who would initiate a conversation with him in the evening unless it was an emergency.

One evening I walked through the mud and sat down on the log next to my friend both of us finishing a cup of coffee. "Phil, are you letting this job get you down?" When the men were out of earshot I often called the major by his first name.

"I don't know Ray. It seems like I didn't have to kill the colonel or let his officers be tortured to death. The war was over, but they had brutally killed innocent civilians here in the jungle. If we had taken them prisoner, we would have had to guard them all the way back to India and share our meager supply of food. It was much easier to kill them, wasn't it? I think our troops would have slit their throats one at a time on our way home anyway."

I stared down at the mud and didn't answer. "You and I have been doing this for almost four years now, Phil, and I have never seen it get to you like this before. What's done is done. Now you have the responsibility of getting us home. Let's concentrate on that." I put my arm on the major's shoulder in a show of affection that the men had not seen before. Phil smiled and nodded in agreement as I rose and walked back to my hammock.

TWENTY-TWO

The morning sun rose with an intensity that caused the mud to dry quickly. The men's spirits were higher, and they walked like it. They recognized the trail from their trip up it several days ago. "I am certainly not looking forward to reaching the spot where we killed the three hundred or so Japanese soldiers earlier this week," I heard Phil say. As we approached the clearing on the side of the mountain, the smell of death permeated the jungle air.

Phil finally stepped out into the familiar clearing and the glare of the bright sunlight hit him in the face. There were no Japanese bodies on the trail where we had left them. No one said anything. One of the sergeants took his backpack off, set his weapon on the trail and slid down the mountain toward the bottom. When he reached the pile of corpses he turned back up to the trail. "Major, these men have all been stripped of their clothing and packs. A poor attempt was made to cover up the bodies, but most are still visible through the mud."

"Hey major," a voice came from about fifty yards down the trail. "All of their weapons are gone, including their ammunition, knives, canteens, swords and binoculars. Everything has been stolen." Phil took off his pack and set it and his weapon on the trail. He sat down on a rock with his legs hanging over the side looking down at the bodies. I sat down beside him.

He turned to me. "Remember Ray, we left the bodies and the weapons here intentionally, planning to take care of them when we came back down the trail. We intended to bury the weapons so that they would not fall into the wrong hands, and look what has happened. In just the four days that we have been gone, someone who was probably following us, moved in and stripped all the weapons and clothes from the dead bodies and made a half-hearted attempt to bury them. Who are these people and what are we up against?"

I just shook my head and stared down the canyon. "I don't know Phil, but whoever it is, they are heavily armed. Who needs so many weapons with the war over? There were three hundred rifles, pistols, submachine guns, knives swords and all of their ammunition. This much weaponry could not have been carried out by a couple of dozen men. This was a large group who wanted to arm themselves."

"Yes, and they have a purpose, whatever it may be," the major added. He turned. "Sergeant!"

"Have the men finish covering the bodies as well as they can and sent out a patrol to see if they can locate tracks or other identifying marks leading away from here."

"My God, what are we facing Ray?" he asked again. "Three hundred heavily armed men are out there under the cover of an impregnable jungle," Phil took out his handkerchief and wiped the perspiration off his face. "I doubt if they are Japanese. Japanese troops would already be armed and would not be so careless in burying their comrades. It must be locals. But why?"

"Phil. Do you suppose that we have wandered into China?" I asked.

"That's a good question Ray. Sergeant, would you please ask our Burmese scout to come back here?"

It took a few minutes to find old what's-his-name. He was out searching for clues in the underbrush and around the hillside. He trotted up and sat down next to the two officers. "Yes Sir, what can I do for you?"

"No Sir, I haven't. But there is still lots of ground to cover."

"I'm wondering, is it possible that we are in China? This trail we have been following turns in all directions, and I know we are near the Chinese border. Could we have crossed into Yunnan Province unintentionally on our trek up here?"

"That's a good question major. I am not familiar with this particular part of Burma, and I don't have a map. It is possible that we strayed back and forth between countries as we've walked along the border. But I doubt if it matters or if the natives who live here know or care."

Phil was lost in thought as he stared off into the distance. "Captain, let's continue down the trail and spend the night in the outpost that Lieutenant Schultz and Lieutenant Hashimoto so effectively wiped out on our way up here. And when we are settled, please bring the men together. I want to tell them what we are up against, at least as far as I know."

TWENTY-THREE

"All right men, here's all I know." The rain had stopped, the campsite was prepared, and the men were ready to eat and sleep for the night. "You all know that the Japanese weapons were stolen by a large group of men whose identities and allegiance we cannot identify. Unfortunately, as we continue down the trail and through the jungle, we are in the most vulnerable military situation possible. A long column of men is easily wiped out as we showed the Japanese four days ago in our brilliant ambush."

The men looked at each other and smiled at the major's description of his own tactics.

"The best historical example of this occurred in the first century when a few hundred native Celtic tribesmen killed eighteen thousand Roman soldiers in Germany's Black Forest. The three legions of Romans were marching along a dense trail in a single column when they were attacked by locals living in the forest. Unfortunately, we have no choice.

"All you can do is keep your weapons handy and be ready to fight at any moment. Don't be trigger-happy. We can't afford to waste ammunition shooting at every rodent we see running through the jungle. We will keep scouts out ahead and sentries posted around us all night. I don't know what is out there, but we can't take chances. Are there any questions? Yes private?"

"Sir, can you tell us what has happened to Nang? We haven't seen her since we left the Japanese camp."

"No, I can't, private. I have not seen nor heard from her either, but I wouldn't worry. She can take care of herself in the jungle." The major did not add that he wished he knew what side she was on and what her agenda was. Those thoughts had been going through his mind ever since they had left her to "watch" the Japanese prisoners.

Major Jenkins had a good night sleep. He covered himself with his tarp just in case, which proved to be a good idea. It showered a little, but the sun broke out from the clouds in the morning as its bright orange hue could be seen on the eastern horizon. The water in the mud soon began to vaporize as the sun warmed it.

"Anybody got an extra cup of coffee?" was the major's way of getting things moving in the morning. A corporal ran up with the major's steaming coffee in his personal cup. He was sitting on a rock pulling on his boots over smelly socks, when he heard a commotion coming from the other side of camp.

"Major! I've found a local tribesman who wants to talk to you," their Burmese scout called as he came running up breathless with a small man in tow. "He says his name is Duwa and he is the chief of a local town. He says he has critical information for you."

"Okay, bring him over, and by the way tell me your name again. I am terrible with names."

"Yes Sir. My name is Aung San," he replied, as the two Burmese men sat down in front of the major.

"Ah yes. And may I call you Aung for short?"

"Of course major, and I need to add that Duwa is not this man's real name, but is the word for Town Chief in Burmese. He insists that we call him that." The major nodded.

"Now what do we have here?" Phil asked as he took another sip of coffee. He studied the small elderly man dressed in a white robe with a colorful sash around his waist.

The two Burmese men talked rapidly to each other for several minutes, then Aung turned to the Major and translated. "Duwa says that we are next to the Chinese border that it is just over that mountain," pointing to the northeast. "He calls them the Kaolikung Mountains. He says that there is a battalion of Chinese Communist soldiers about five miles from here, and they are the ones who stole the Japanese weapons. They heard the gunfire when you ambushed the troops and came running over as you and your men resumed marching up the mountain."

The major nodded and looked over at me as I was now standing nearby. He returned his gaze to the scout. "Yes. Go on."

"He says that now that the war with Japan is over, the Chinese Communist Army intends to take over Yunnan Province, but they had no weapons until you came along. Now they are fully armed and spoiling for a fight."

"Yes, but we have no axe to grind with them. What does this all have to do with us?" I asked.

"They do not look at it that way, captain. Your Army supported the Chinese Nationalists in their fight against Japan, and they think you are now the enemy. Remember, the Chinese Communist Army fought very little against the Japanese during the past ten years. They were waiting for the Nationalist Army to wear itself out fighting the invaders. When the war was over, they would arm themselves, strike at Chung Kai-shek and wipe out all his troops. Their time would have come.

"You may not have an axe to grind with them, captain, but you have a duty to your men to protect them from attack by a superior enemy force that does have an axe to grind with you." Now I looked over at the major who was trying to hide his concern.

"Al right you guys, calm down. Let's talk about how we can get ourselves out of this situation alive," Phil finally broke in.

"He has other news, major. He says that his spies tell him that the Communist brigade is forming over that mountain with their new weapons and are planning to attack us first thing tomorrow morning. They are more numerous than we, and they are planning to wipe us out in one lightning strike."

There were several minutes of silence as the officers tried to envision how they would protect themselves against such an attack. The two Burmese continued talking between themselves. The scout turned to the major.

"Duwa wants me to tell you that there is a way to defend yourselves against this attack." All the men within earshot stared at the major. He looked at his scout and asked, "Okay, tell me how."

"About two miles down the hill, the trail splits, and the right or eastern fork continues into Yunnan Province. The left or western fork is the one you will take to get back to India. If you take the eastern fork, you will soon come to a bridge that crosses a deep gorge before it reaches the Chinese border. The Communist Army will cross that bridge on its way to attack.

"If you wish to protect yourselves, I suggest that you set explosive charges on this bridge, wait until their army is on it and blow it up. Not only will you wipe out the immediate threat to your unit, you will set up a barrier to any further incursion of Chinese Communists into Burma. That bridge is their only access to our country for fifty miles in either direction. You must set the charges today, as they plan to cross it in the morning."

We exchanged glances. "Is that all Aung?" Phil asked. Aung replied. "He says that you Americans are their only protection against this large Communist force, and he hopes that you will take his suggestion and defend the women and children of his village," Duwa and the scout bowed and turned to walk away. The major scratched his growing beard.

Major Jenkins turned to his sergeant major and asked, "Sergeant, are our explosives in usable condition?"

"Yes Sir. They are ready to go." The major nodded and turned to me.

"What do you think Ray?"

"The decision is yours, of course, Phil," I offered. " "But I don't see that we have a choice. There is no way out of this jungle unless we can deploy our men in such a way that we could defeat a heavily armed force coming out of China. We would be slaughtered as you correctly have pointed out to us."

The major turned to his sergeant major. "Sergeant, please have the charges loaded onto mules and get the men ready to move out. We are going to find that bridge."

"Yes Sir."

TWENTY-FOUR

The sergeant major was in charge of the men setting the explosives, and I supervised the operation as I walked back and forth along the bridge. Major Jenkins sat on the hillside next to the bridge watching the process. He was an expert in explosives and in bridge structures and once in a while, he would advise me to put a bigger charge in place or move it up to a more vulnerable location. But in general, he was happy with what he saw.

"Hey Ray! Look how this bridge is designed. As I recall, it is called a rigid frame design with inclined legs. The four legs are inclined about forty-five degrees from the bridge structure down where they connect into the walls of the canyon."

Pointing at them, he continued, "These four legs take the compressive live load from people and carts traveling across the bridge and are the logical structures to be destroyed in the explosion. The explosives must be placed in the center of the legs where the buckling stress is the highest." Our men were well trained and knew how to put the explosives in exactly the right spot. "Captain, be sure that the wires are run all the way back into the jungle several hundred feet to the detonator. We don't want the Chinese soldiers to see us from the bridge," the major said.

"Yes Sir."

The men were suspended down each side of the bridge by ropes tied around their waists and held by their buddies up on the bridge roadway. It was just wide enough for a cart pulled by two mules or four men walking abreast. The 50-yard bridge spanned the canyon, which was about one hundred-fifty yards above the stream that ran along the bottom of the gorge.

"Didn't they do a beautiful job of building this bridge, Ray," the major asked me while I stood in the center of the span looking down at the gorge. I nodded and commented, "It's a shame that we have to blow it. Look how they have used bamboo as the load bearing timber and lashed it together with jungle vines at just the right spots. They seem to have a inherent understanding of stress and loading that we can't even imagine."

It wasn't long before the explosives were tied in place, and the men were lifted up onto the bridge roadway. They walked back toward the Burmese side of the bridge joking with each other while stringing electrical wire and covering it with a layer of dirt to hide it from enemy scouts. They walked back into the jungle and tied off the wires in preparation to their connection to the detonator box. "Let's leave them here and we'll connect the wires when we arrive in the morning before the Communists get here," Phil said.

"What time do we expect them to arrive tomorrow, major," the sergeant major asked.

"Our Burmese informant says that his spies tell him they will be here shortly after dawn. If we get here at dawn, that should be enough time to make the final preparations and deploy the men for battle."

"Do we expect to fight after blowing up the bridge, sir?"

"No, I don't sergeant. I think that the bridge collapse will kill them all, but we must be prepared for anything."

The major turned to me and said, "You seem more subdued than usual Ray. Is something bothering you?"

"No Phil, not really. I'm just trying to be sure that we haven't missed anything." However, I'm sure that the look on my face probably told him a different story. Phil nodded, ignoring my expression.

The men packed up the mules and headed back to camp for their evening meal and a sound sleep. It hadn't rained all day, and the ground was drying up fast in the jungle heat. The monsoon season was nearing an end. That night, they all slept soundly. I was the only exception as I spent several hours staring up at the starry sky and sliver of a moon. There was something about this whole operation that was bothering me, but I couldn't put my finger on it. We were preparing to kill several hundred people at the request of an informant, who we didn't know, for the protection of our troops who were trying to get home after the end of a terrible war. Why didn't this make sense? I finally fell asleep unable to provide an answer.

TWENTY-FIVE

The eastern sky was showing some light as the men crouched down in their hiding places at the edge of the jungle. They were all sitting with their weapons across their laps, so they could see the bridge and watch the fireworks.

The major, along with the sergeant major and I, were in a small clearing next to the trail as it wandered out onto the bridge. We were far enough into the jungle to be well hidden. It would be the sergeant major's job to activate the detonator when the major gave the order. We all waited nervously staring into the eastern mountains searching for our adversary.

"I hear something." The sound of men marching through the jungle on the east side of the canyon was getting louder by the minute. The sergeant major gripped the handle on his detonator, and Phil raised himself a little higher to peer over the jungle undergrowth. Now he could make out figures in the dark coming toward the bridge. "I can see them!"

He raised his arm in preparation. It was still too dark to identify the oncoming army, but he realized that we had only one chance. Now the enemy began to march out onto the bridge in what appeared to be a four across column.

Phil waited until they reached the near end of the bridge, not quite clear of it, and he dropped his arm. The explosion rocked the canyon with an ear splitting roar. A huge column of smoke and fire shot up obscuring the bridge but not drowning out the screams of the occupants as they fell several hundred feet to their deaths.

As silence returned, the smoke lingered over the gorge blanking out the stream below. The three men stood up and looked across the canyon to the north side to see if there were any soldiers remaining. "I don't see any movement," I said. "I think we got them all."

The men slowly rose from their hiding places and walked to the canyon's edge looking down at the jumble of wood and bodies in the river mostly hidden by smoke. It was all over.

"Take two men with you and repel down the canyon wall to the bottom; make sure they are all dead and check the uniforms on those soldiers. I want to know what Chinese unit they are with."

We all watched with interest as the three men were lowered down the wall into the small stream running along the bottom. The smoke was beginning to clear when they reached the canyon base and untied the ropes around their waists.

The three men walked between the bodies spread out on the rocks. The sergeant stopped and turned looking up. "Major! These people are not Chinese Communist soldiers. They are all Burmese civilians, men, women and children!"

A stunned silence fell over the troops. I stared blindly out across the canyon. Our men looked at Phil for answers, but he had none.

"Get Duwa over here immediately! The major shouted. "He left as soon as the charge went off," a soldier said. Phil was suddenly overcome as tears came to his eyes and poured down his cheeks. I joined him.

TWENTY-SIX

"What have we done, Ray?" The two of us were sitting on a log back from the edge of the canyon so we couldn't see down to the bottom. The three soldiers were being lifted up out of the gorge as we both sat there with tears running down our cheeks. Neither of us could answer Phil's rhetorical question. But we had to come up with an answer. The men demanded it.

They didn't say anything, but they didn't have to. No one looked at the major. They were all afraid their eyes would meet.

Then we heard a noise coming out of the jungle behind us. Each man reached for his weapon instinctively, and then sat them down as we saw Nang running along the trail toward us. And she was screaming. "Maybe we can get some answers," I said hopefully.

Nang came to an abrupt halt in front of the two of us, and turning to look at the demolished bridge, put her hands on her hips, and then looked down at the bottom of the gorge. She slowly turned back toward us. We were all now trying to wipe our eyes. "I thought I would have to ask what has happened here, but I can see," Nang said.

"You two fools have been taken in by Duwa haven't you?" Before either of us could answer, she continued. "I cannot believe it. He has made you do his dirty work, hasn't he?" Again, we had two open mouths, but nothing came out.

"You damn fools! Do you know who Duwa is? He is the leader of a pro-Japanese band of Burmese guerillas who have been living in a village near here. He was fighting against the English before the

Japanese came and rushed to join forces with the Japanese invaders. He led his supporters north along the Irrawaddi, until they came into contact with Colonel Maruyama's band of Japanese killers. The colonel was not happy to have Duwa following him around, but he tolerated them as the Japanese moved up here into the jungle. But Burmese villagers would not let Duwa and his supporters stay with them more than overnight, at least not until they reached a little village about five miles up that ridge over there.

"When the villagers heard that Colonel Maruyama's troops were headed their way, they all fled across the bridge that you just blew up and camped out in China waiting for the war to end.

"When Duwa and his followers reached the then empty town, they took it over and have lived there for the past year. Their big problem surfaced when the war ended, and it was obvious that the original villagers would return and attempt to re-claim their homes. Fortunately for Duwa, when you guys came marching down the trail, he saw his chance. He thought he could convince you to blow up this bridge and keep out his enemies, maybe killing them all. He didn't realize how efficient your men are.

"So you did his bidding, and several hundred Burmese civilians now lie dead at the bottom of the gorge, and this centuries-old bridge no longer exists. Trade with our Chinese neighbors east of here is no longer possible. You probably don't even know what that means for our survival now that the war is over."

"We thought they were Communists," I chimed in weakly.

"You idiots thought they were Communists?" Nang responded. "You know nothing about history. Most of the Communists in Yunnan Province left with the Long March in 1936. It was in Yunnan Province that the march started you know. There aren't a dozen active Communists left in the entire province! When are you Americans going to read history books?"

Nang put her head in her hands and sobbed. The men who were listening looked away. It wasn't appropriate for soldiers to be seen crying. No one could think of what to say. They all thought of the tremendous power of destruction they had in their hands. No one stopped to consider the consequences of using all that power. It just seemed like the appropriate thing to do.

They all looked at the major. He had made the decision to blow up the bridge and kill all these people. They also knew that he did what he thought was necessary to protect his men. But hadn't there been some way to confirm that what Duwa had just told them was correct before killing so many people?

And where was Nang when we needed her? Phil thought. She could have prevented this, but she was not here. None dared to ask her; she was obviously not one to be trifled with, especially with my bowie knife strapped to her waist. Nang rose from her log perch and walked over to the edge of the canyon and looked down at the still smoking pile of bodies over one hundred feet below them. She turned to look at the major. "It looks like Colonel Maruyama has had the last laugh, major." She turned to look down at her dead countrymen for the last time then turned again and walked back along the trail away from the smoking ruins of the centuries old bridge.

TWENTY-SEVEN

The major had no stomach for dinner. He sat staring into the small campfire the corporal had built for him. It wasn't cold enough for a fire, but it reminded him of the times he had spent hunting with his father in the California Mountains. He couldn't look up. "As I said before Phil, what's done is done. We have to concentrate now on getting out of this jungle alive," I reminded him.

"Yes, I know Ray."

Nang was sitting close by finishing her bowl of rice. The major turned to her. "So Colonel Maruyama tells me that you are a terrorist." Everyone thought that it was strange that he used the present tense, like the colonel was still talking to him.

"One man's terrorist is the next man's freedom fighter," she responded with a smile. "No, I didn't tell you everything, because I didn't think you needed to know. Yes, Colonel Maruyama and I had met before, several times as a matter of fact. I almost killed him several weeks ago when our guerilla group hit him about ten miles down the road from here. I thought he was the most vulnerable at that point.

"Unfortunately, he was more skilled than I thought, and he rallied his men into a defensive position that we could not penetrate, and he escaped. When you came along, I saw my chance. I must say that you and your men are the most efficient killers I have ever seen, and I have seen a lot in the years we have been fighting the English and

Japanese." Phil and I looked at her and then at each other with some satisfaction.

"So where is your guerilla group now?" the major asked not expecting an answer.

"When you need to know, I will tell you," Nang replied. She was now in complete control of the situation, as she leaned back and finished her tea.

Ignoring her curt reply, the major continued. "And who stole the Japanese weapons? Duwa?"

"Yes, of course. My people have plenty of weapons, some stolen from the English and some from the Japanese. So now a large group of jungle fighters, sympathetic to the Japanese, are also armed to the teeth. And the chance of you confronting them in a battle that would allow you to wipe them out is nearly zero. As you know Major, your group is very vulnerable, perhaps more than you realize.

"But you have an even bigger problem. Your massacre of innocent civilians this morning will enrage the locals when they hear about it. In fact, the word is spreading fast as we speak. I don't know what action they will take to inflict revenge on you, but it won't be pleasant."

"There are no accidents in war, captain. We have been fighting various enemies since the Chinese first invaded our homeland several hundred years ago. And we had certainly been fighting the English for almost one hundred years until the Japanese came and ran them off. You Americans are just the latest version."

"That's ridiculous, Nang. We are not English, and we have no intention of staying here now that the war is over," Phil replied.

"But you have one very important disadvantage, Major. You are white and look just like the English. You even wear those stupid Australian hats with one brim tied up against the top. Our people are not sophisticated enough to recognize the difference. Every foreigner in our country today is an enemy, including the Indian troops your English friends use as cannon fodder."

No use arguing with her, the major thought. "So, tell us Nang. How did you get involved in this war?"

With a severe look in her eyes that Major Jenkins had not seen before, she responded, "I grew up on a rice plantation owned by my parents that had been in our family for generations. It was located on the Irrawaddi Delta just north of Rangoon. The flood plane along the Irrawaddi for its entire thousand-mile journey from the Himalayas is one of the most fertile regions in the Middle East. We grew plenty of rice for export, often with some left over for our neighbors.

"Unfortunately, most Burmese didn't have enough income to pay for the rice they grew, so our English overlords sold much of the crop to India and kept the profit for themselves. However, the English didn't invent this thievery. It began with Chinese and continued with the Japanese when they threw out the English. We Burmese are tired of bullies stealing our food from us, much less taking our natural resources. I won't even go into that.

"Many Burmese thought that the Japanese, as they are also Asians, would give us the freedom and independence we so badly wished for. They even invited our leader, Dr. Ba Ma, to Tokyo in 1943 to talk with Japanese leaders about their 'Greater East Asia Co-prosperity Sphere.' Of course nothing came of that, and we learned that the Japanese troops were just as brutal as any invaders we had seen.

"So we are more than a little suspicious of any army that comes marching in to Burma to 'save' its people. You just happen to be the latest version, even though you profess no ambitions here. If what you say is true, you are just a victim of bad timing.

"Remember, when our previous conquerors came here, they were supported by thousands of combat troops fully equipped with the latest weapons. Your troops, on the other hand, are small in number and have only a few machine guns, mortars, rifles and submachine guns. Again I say, you are just in the wrong place at the wrong time."

No one spoke for a while, until the major broke in with, "Can you help us get out of Burma, Nang?"

She stared at him for a minute, and then said, "You don't seem to understand the predicament you are in major. To answer your question, I don't know. But your real question should be do I want to help you get out of Burma? Then your follow up question should be, will I help you get out of Burma? "When you marched up this mountain range a few weeks ago to capture and kill Colonel Maruyama and his men, you had only one problem, finding and killing the Japanese. You succeeded with amazing skill. So at the moment the war has ended, your enemy has been defeated and you are home free, so to speak.

"But since that day, you have acquired three more serious problems keeping you from getting back to India. First to consider is the now heavily armed pro-Japanese elements here in the Burmese jungle. In addition, you are facing the anti colonialist segments of the civilian militia, which is pretty much all of Burma right now. Finally, because of your stupidity in listening to Duwa and killing Burmese villagers, you have angered the local people who now want to take revenge on the troops who killed their neighbors. That pretty much identifies every Burmese living within a hundred miles of where you are now sitting. Getting you out of this country alive will be a small miracle that even I may not be able to perform."

The men within hearing distance leaned on their weapons and stared down at the mud; the major and I looked at each other. It was too late to wonder why we had not verified Duwa's information before blowing up the bridge.

"But we didn't have time, and if we had allowed the people to cross the bridge and they had been Chinese Communist soldiers bent on our destruction, we wouldn't be here to talk about it. We have to chalk the event up to one of the tragedies of war," Major Jenkins replied,

Is he rationalizing a failure on his part to take appropriate precautions? I wondered. I know that he probably can't shake Colonel Maruyama's words. Will they haunt him forever? He looked at me, and I wondered if he was thinking the same thing. No, he is probably wondering how to get the hell out of here alive.

"So, Nang, you told us where you were from, but you didn't tell us how and why you came here to Northern Burma up from the delta area. That's almost a thousand miles, over some rough terrain," I asked.

Nang thought a minute, wondering how much she should tell us. "Well, basically the colonel was right. I am a terrorist. At least that is what both the English and Japanese troops thought. When I saw how foreigners were stealing from our country, I organized resistance groups all along the Irrawaddi north almost to the China/India border. When the Japanese Army invaded in force, we could see that we would have to retreat to the mountains and jungles and could only hit them on the edges, as guerillas. So we have been living off the land for over two years now, striking when it was right to do so, and retreating into the jungle when it was appropriate.

"Unfortunately, Colonel Maruyama wiped out almost all of my troops when he led me into a trap a couple weeks ago. I am not as skilled a warrior as you two and fell for his trap. Four of us survived, and I fled up here deep into the jungle to hide. Then I saw you hiking up the trail obviously searching for the colonel, and I hitched a ride. My three compatriots are out recruiting more soldiers, so my band will be up to strength soon. I think you know the rest."

TWENTY-EIGHT

At the first light the next morning, Nang walked over to the clearing where we were sitting, drinking coffee and talking about the trip ahead. She walked as if she were a ballet dancer, slipping through the underbrush and around the trees with the grace associated with a dancer. She has lived in this jungle most of her life, Phil thought as he watched her approach. She nodded a good morning and sat down on a dry rock across from them. She obviously had something on her mind.

"I have become attached to you stupid Americans," she opened the conversation. "The more I think about it, the less chance I see of you getting out of here alive. The only chance you have is to solve each of your three problems one at a time. So let's look at the Duwa problem first.

"He is leading a group of Burmese civilians in an attempt to cut you off and kill you as you walk along the trail." I opened my mouth, but before anything came out, she continued. "Why would he want to kill you, you ask? Remember what I told you last evening. He is a Burmese extension of Colonel Maruyama.

"You Americans don't realize how much we Burmese hated the English over the years. This hatred was translated into support for the Japanese who ran them out. Many of our people overlooked the massacres, killings and kidnappings by the Japanese soldiers. They concentrated only on the fact that the English were gone. Duwa has convinced his people that you Americans, as enemies of the Japanese, are also enemies of the Burmese people.

"His group has one main advantage over you Americans. They know the jungle and how to fight in it. But you have a big advantage over them. You are trained soldiers, and they are civilians. You know how to deploy, attack and retreat when necessary. You know military tactics. We Burmese know how to grow rice and raise children." Phil and I looked at each other thinking about Colonel Maruyama.

"You also have another advantage you don't even know about. I have friends in Duwa's army, and they have kept me informed of his plan of attack." She picked up a stick and moved closer to the two officers. "What is it that they teach you at West Point? That knowing the enemy's plans is ninety percent of winning the battle?"

"So what are their plans for our annihilation," I asked her.

"They have none, at least not yet. They plan to follow you and see if you present an easy target. They have the highest regard for your fighting skills and don't want to go head-to-head with your force, because they fear high casualties."

The major asked, "Is this the only force we have to contend with now?"

"Yes, for the time being, but don't get your hopes up. There are two other armed militia groups out there waiting their turn. Just hope that they don't join forces. Together, they could wipe you out in an hour. I suggest that you just proceed down the trail toward the Irrawaddi and see what happens. I will keep you informed of their progress as my informants tell me."

She rose, smiled at us, and disappeared back into the jungle. Silence permeated the camp as our men contemplated their future while finishing their breakfast. Now every soldier was wondering whose side Nang was really on.

TWENTY-NINE

"Major, may I speak to you for a moment?" It was Sergeant Major Kelly walking up to the two of us as we were all packing and loading up for the day's hike down the trail. Being the senior non-commissioned officer in the unit, it was his responsibility to keep the officers apprised of the condition of the men and to pass on the major's orders to everyone.

"Sure sergeant. What's up?"

"Several things, Sir. First of all, we are getting dangerously low on food. We have gone through most of the food we took from the Japanese camp, and some of it has spoiled in the rain. I would say that we have three days of food left if we cut down on our rations."

The major turned to me and scowled. He waited for the second problem.

"Also, some of the men are getting trench foot from walking in the mud. Army boots are only so good at keeping out the water. Many have given up trying to keep their feet dry entirely. I would suggest, Sir, that we slow the pace a bit so that we can all keep up. Otherwise some toes and maybe some feet are going have to be amputated. We don't have the strength to carry out a few dozen men on stretchers."

"Yes, you are right sergeant. We will slow down the pace a bit. Also, have the men keep a sharp eye out for the deer that live in the jungle. They are very good to eat and you have my permission to shoot one or two for dinner. Don't waste ammunition though."

"Also, we can eat our mules if we have to." Everyone within earshot scowled.

"And by the way sergeant. Please ask Lieutenant Hashimoto to come back here."

We finished loading our packs as Lieutenant Hashimoto trotted up

"Yes, I do lieutenant. I want Captain Beltrans to walk here with me at the rear of the column, so I would like you to take the van position and lead us down the trail. Be sure to keep our Burmese scout at your side at all times and slow that pace down a bit."

"Yes Sir," the lieutenant replied with a smile. It was an honor and sign of confidence to be given the lead position in an Army unit. He turned and trotted back to the head of the column as the men loaded their packs on their backs and smiled at him as he went by.

In battle zones, enlisted men or junior officers do not salute the senior officers as they would in the states. If an enemy were watching, he would know that the man being saluted was an officer and would probably aim his fire at him.

"I wish we knew for sure if we could trust Nang," I said with some apprehension.

"Yes, I have been wondering the same thing," Phil replied. "There is obviously a great deal she is not telling us, but that may be for a good reason. Still, it would be nice if her intentions were all out on the table where we could see them. But maybe if we knew what we were up against, we would all die of fright."

I remember that I was not amused. "So let's just go with what we have, and do the best we can."

We had been walking a couple of hours when the column stopped, and a loud commotion could be heard coming from the front. The major soon heard a shout for his presence at the head of the column. He and I weaved our way through the exhausted men as they sat down, happy for a chance to rest.

Lieutenant Hashimoto pointed a few feet above their heads at a big jungle tree a short distance off the trail. They looked up.

The Burmese scout was standing next to the trunk. "That, gentlemen, is a dead monkey, killed and nailed to the trunk."

We all stood wide-eyed, staring at a small animal that had recently died in great pain hanging from the tree. No one spoke for a while.

"Okay, what are we looking at?" the major finally asked.

The scout turned to us frowning. "This is an ancient Burmese warning given to their enemies. It is telling us that they intend to kill us all."

After a few minutes of silence, "Who are these people?" Phil asked.

"I told you who these people are major. They are Duwa and his band of Japanese sympathizers who are angry that you killed their friend, Colonel Maruyama." We all turned in time to see Nang appear through the jungle behind us.

"They have decided how to kill you and are now trying to instill a level of terror in you before they attack. Remember, a fearful enemy is a beaten enemy. Let's keep moving, and I will explain to you as we walk."

"Lieutenant Hashimoto, continue on the trail, and keep your eyes open, especially in the trees," the major ordered.

"Yes Sir." The lieutenant motioned for the men to get up and follow him with the scout walking beside him. With audible groans, the men rose to their sore feet, threw their weapons over their shoulders and continued their slow march through the jungle.

THIRTY

The three of us, the major, Nang and I walked together at the rear of the column in silence. As we progressed deeper into the jungle, and the altitude dropped, the weather became hotter and muggier. It was nice to have the Monsoon over, but now the air became more stifling and unbearable. The mosquitoes were as big as birds or at least they seemed to be.

The men began peeling off clothes one by one, unconcerned with Nang's presence. Nothing seemed to help. As they now walked through puddles of standing water, they became more aware of increasing swarms of mosquitoes around them. "Put your shirts back on to protect yourselves from the millions of mosquitoes that love your skin and want your blood," the sergeant major ordered. The men slowly complied with the sergeant's order but not without grumbling.

After a while, I couldn't stand it any longer and asked "So what are we facing Nang?"

"It looks like the attack won't be before tomorrow, so I will give you the details when we are in camp."

Then we all heard it! A chilling scream that penetrated through the jungle. Everyone stopped in his tracks and stared ahead waiting for the next sound. Then came a single shot obviously fired from a .45 pistol. The three of us at the back end of the column took our weapons off our shoulders and began running toward the front, the soldiers standing aside as we hurried past.

We rounded a bend and halted next to the Burmese scout, sergeant major and several soldiers all staring down at the ground. Lieutenant Hashimoto was lying on the ground writhing in pain, clutching his leg and screaming in anguish. The scout had a smoking pistol in his right hand. He was looking down at the lieutenant and pointing to the underbrush next to the trail with his left hand. On the ground, lying coiled up and without a head they could make out a large King Cobra, the deadliest snake in the jungle. It must have been six or eight feet long. "What happened?" the Major asked, although it was becoming more apparent as they stood there in horror.

Before anyone could answer, the unit medic came running up to the group, pushed us all aside and dropped his bag on the ground. He rolled the lieutenant over on his back and ripped his pant leg open. There everyone could see the two deadly teeth marks made by a poisonous snake. Blood was oozing out as the lieutenant cried out.

The medic pulled out his knife and began slicing into the lieutenant's leg, trying to increase the bleeding in hopes that the blood would bring the poison out with it. The others grabbed the lieutenant to hold him still so that the corporal could do the work he was trained for, but the incisions didn't seem to be helping. The major, with tears in his eyes, turned around to look at Nang, but she shook her head sadly and looked away from him. "No one has ever been known to survived a bite from the jungle King Cobra," she said softly while walking away.

THIRTY-ONE

We had given Lieutenant Hashimoto as good a Christian burial as we could manage in the jungle. He had not been a Christian very long, having grown up attending his parents' Buddhist temple in San Francisco. He had been converted only recently by a Catholic priest when he joined the Army. We fashioned a cross from bamboo stocks, lashed them together and sunk it into the soft and still wet ground.

Major Jenkins presided at the burial as commanding officers have done for millennia. He was not very religious, but he loved his lieutenant and gave him a rousing send off. The men loved it too, and all had tears in their eyes as he finished.

Our officers and Nang were all sitting around camp after our now sparse dinner. "There is something very strange about this," the major said. "We have been three months in this jungle and haven't seen any cobras. Yet we know they live all around us."

"Yes, they can hear us coming and will always slither out of our way before we get to them," Nang broke in. "They don't like us any more than we like them." After a short pause, "This was not a chance encounter. I think that he was planted there just before Lieutenant Hashimoto arrived."

All of our officers looked at Nang with disbelief. "There are Burmese who keep cobras as pets. Yes, it can be dangerous, but it is considered a mark of distinction and bravery to keep a pet cobra. However, they often let them go when they get that big. I believe that this one was brought to the trail by his owner, set free and given food, probably mice or rats, to keep him in the right spot for a few minutes until Lieutenant Hashimoto walked up. It was a good thing that our scout was quick on the draw, or he might have been killed too."

Our officers looked at one another each of us wondering if any of us would sleep tonight.

"We call the cobra a naja, which is actually the name of a species to which all cobras belong. You may not know this, but cobras are so plentiful here in Burma that we actually eat them. They are a real delicacy."

Now the men were beginning to get sick. Some wandered off before they heard more.

"These are vicious people," I responded looking down at the ground.

"No, they are not captain. They are civilians, men and women with children, probably strapped to their backs. They can and do hate after several hundred years of maltreatment at the hands of foreigners, and they use the only weapons available. They don't have access to the modern weapons that you have, except when they steal them. So they fight with what they have, as if their lives depended on it, which it often does. They just happen to hate you more because you killed their friends, the Japanese. They think you will bring the English back."

After a long pause, the major asked Nang, "Okay, what about tomorrow? You said that our enemy might attack us sometime tomorrow. Is that true?"

"Yes it is major. They have been tracking you since you blew up the bridge and have finally selected your graveyard. Duwa is leading them into position as we speak so that you will march into their trap tomorrow, rather like the one you sprang on your Japanese enemies.

"About five miles down the trail is a clearing in the jungle through which you will have to cross. It is an opening that will expose your entire unit to a murderous crossfire. They learned well from you.

"I suggest that you allow some of your troops to cross into the meadow, but move most of your men around to the left behind the enemy. They will wait to see that all of your troops are exposed before they open fire, so you should be able to get well behind them without endangering any of your men. If you time it just right, you can wipe them out before they begin firing on your exposed group in the meadow. How does that sound?"

"How does it make sense to kill women with children on their backs who are trying to kill us because we killed their friends, the Japs? They never taught us this at the academy," I responded.

"Okay men. You have to forget that they are civilians. They are your sworn enemy, intent on your destruction. You have about one hundred-fifty soldiers who are depending on you officers to bring them out of this jungle alive. These civilians have already killed one of your top officers, and you are wondering if it's moral? What planet do you fools live on?" No one offered to answer her question.

"What do you think, Phil?" I finally asked after the rest went off to their respective sleeping bags and hammocks.

"I don't know Ray. Is she really on our side or are we being led into a trap? Let's think for a moment how she could attack us."

"Well, she could place her troops, or some of them behind us so that when we opened fire, her people could attack suddenly from our rear, or flank,"

"That's a real possibility, Ray. I think we need to take all necessary precautions. Let's put some troops in our rear facing away from us to warn if there is an attack."

"I agree that we must prepare for any possibility, Phil. I just can't believe that she would be telling us how to kill her countrymen."

THIRTY-TWO

"Okay, gather round men!"

The sergeants and officers moved up close to Major Jenkins so they could hear his orders. The sun broke bright that morning, and the sky was a clear blue reminding everyone that they were getting close to home.

"There is a clearing, a meadow, a few miles down the trail. Lieutenant Schultz, I want you to take the lead, and with your platoon, strike out across it like nothing was wrong. Have your weapons cocked and ready for action. When you hear the first shots, drop immediately to the ground and look to your left. That is where the action should be taking place. If you see appropriate targets open up, but don't expose your men needlessly. Do you understand?"

"When we get within sight of the meadow, Captain Beltrans will lead the rest of our unit around it to the left, staying out of sight in the jungle. We are assuming that there is an army on our left flank ready to ambush us when you appear in the open. But, of course, we will not all be in the meadow. We will be behind them and will open fire when Captain Beltrans thinks that it is appropriate.

"Lieutenant, you and your men will be their targets if they start firing. Your survival may depend on your ability to fall to the ground before their bullets reach you."

I thought that it was interesting that my friend referred to the enemy as an "army" and not a group of civilians.

The major turned to one of his staff sergeants and said, "Sergeant, I want you to select six good men, and when we reach our firing position on the left, you and your men will turn away from us, walk out about a hundred yards, and watch for any enemy that might attack us from our rear. If you spot anyone coming at us from behind or toward our flank, fire your weapons once and then return to us on the run. You won't be able to hold them off, but your fire will alert us that we are being attacked from our rear. Is that clear? There will be no talking from anyone unless it is an order or a sighting."

"Okay. Let's move out." He looked around, but Nang was nowhere to be seen.

It didn't take long to get to the meadow, but the major noticed on the way that a few of his men were limping, some badly. He thought he saw that some men were shivering. "But it's not cold," he said as he turned to me.

Standing back, he saw Lieutenant Schultz and his platoon move out cautiously across the meadow and watched me motion my men to our left while still back in the jungle. He brought up the rear. I think I have considered everything, he mused to himself.

Staying in the jungle and walking silently, we soon reached a spot where we could see the thinning trees along the edge, a good spot for the ambushing enemy to be out of sight and still see the meadow. Phil could see Lieutenant Schultz and his men slowly walking across the meadow looking in all directions with their weapons up and ready to fire. He thought that their attention to their surroundings might give away their plan.

Leading my men, I suddenly stopped and dropped down. I saw something in the brush but could not identify it. I raised my hand, and my men stopped and fell to the ground. The staff sergeant and his six men turned and started running quietly to their rear. Very good so far, the major thought.

The men slowly crawled up to form a firing line on each side of me, staying low and out of sight. The major was too far behind us to tell what we were looking at, but we were all very attentive to what was in front of us. Major Jenkins was getting nervous. I am sure he was wondering, why doesn't Ray open fire? What I saw in front of us shocked me, and I lay there in the bushes transfixed. I couldn't tell him without revealing our position. There was no sign language for what I saw in front of us.

I rose up and looked back at Phil with a quizzical expression. Now what is going on, Phil thought as he stared back at me and motioned for me to start firing. I did what he was ordered but knew that we would soon regret it.

Sergeant O'Rourke and his six soldiers moved quickly through the trees to their assigned positions behind the unit. The grass was thick so they lowered themselves quietly to the ground and crawled the last few feet on hands and knees.

Just before reaching their assigned position, they heard a hissing sound in front of them. They stopped in horror as a large cobra rose up out of the grass. The sergeant motioned for them not to fire at it. An enemy force out there would be alerted to their presence by gunfire. Thinking about Sergeant Hashimoto, the men had trouble hiding their terror. With the calmness of a professional boxer, the sergeant quickly reached to his left and pulled a long machete knife from his waistband and swung it at the snake. With little effort, the razor sharp blade cut the cobra in two just below its flattened head. The men let out a sigh of relief.

In a couple of minutes, they reached their position at the edge of a small clearing. They stopped and looked out across the clearing to the jungle edge and sat down to keep watch on the area as the major had ordered.

After a while, Private Johnson turned to the sergeant, and in a loud whisper said, "Hey sarge, did you see that?"

"Over there. Look on the right side of that clump of trees. I thought I saw something move."

"I don't see anything Johnson. But keep your eyes peeled."

They kept looking, afraid to blink, but saw nothing more. Then they heard the firing begin behind them.

THIRTY-THREE

The men under my leadership were accurate and deadly killers. They did not waste ammunition and almost every bullet hit someone. The major even added a few of his own shots at several men he saw trying to escape around the edge. The enemy's firing was sporadic and ineffective which amazed all of us. They were obviously surprised and confused by the direction of the fire. They had expected to engage the soldiers in the meadow but had no idea that most of the Americans were behind them. They were apparently not well trained and thus unable to shift their fire toward their real threat behind them.

It was short and deadly. The major soon stood up and waved for Staff Sergeant O'Rourke and his six men to return to the group. The sergeant reported to the major that they had seen nothing, at least nothing that they could verify. He didn't report that he had cut a cobra in two, but the major noticed that his machete had blood running down its blade.

At least no one had attacked them from the rear. The men on the firing line soon rose up and walked to their dead enemy to see who they were. The major noticed that some of them began to throw up. "Now what?" he asked to no one in particular.

He walked up to the skirmish line and saw what they were all looking at. Looking down, he saw close to a hundred old men, women of all ages, and children from teen age down to babies. Most of them had been killed outright. Some were in the process of dying.

Many of his men were sitting on the ground sobbing. Our medic was running among the casualties trying to find someone he could patch up, someone who might survive. He too had tears running down his cheeks.

In the middle of the men, Phil finally saw me staring back at him. "This is why you waved at me," he said. "You saw what we were up against. And this is why their firing was so ineffective. They are just civilians with no military training." I kept looking at him; he couldn't bear to look down at the pile of dead humanity.

"Hey major. We have a wounded man here who wants to talk to you," the sergeant major yelled at him. The major shouldered his tommy gun, wiped his cheeks and walked over to see what this was about. He approached Duwa lying in a pool of blood. The major looked down at him and shook his head.

"You damn fool. Leading these people into a fight that you couldn't possibly win." He waved his arm back over the dead and dying. "These civilians don't know which end of the gun the bullets comes out of. Even if we hadn't come in behind you, we would have won in the end. You deserved what you got."

His men looked over at him with surprise. "Okay, maybe I didn't mean that," he said softly.

"How did you know that we would be here?" Duwa coughed up blood as he spoke. "Oh wait. You had a spy in our group didn't you? No, you couldn't have had a spy. Oh yes, I know. It was Nang, the famous Burmese terrorist, wasn't it? I should have killed her when I had a chance several months ago. But no, I let her go. What harm could a cute little Burmese girl do to any of us? I guess I've found," out he said as he continued to spit up blood.

The major took his weapon off his shoulder and knelt down, so Duwa could hear him better. "You are now responsible for the death of four or five hundred civilians," Phil said with bitterness in his voice. "Oh yes, you got us to do your dirty work but the irony is that we are only trying to get home, and leave this bloody country to you who live here."

Duwa smiled slightly as he coughed up more blood. "You still don't get it do you major? We were all sympathetic to the Japanese because they ran out the hated English, as Nang probably told you. When you wiped out Colonel Maruyama and his men, it left us exposed and vulnerable. All the other guerilla groups in this jungle now consider us to be the enemy, and since the colonel is gone, who will protect us? We are at the mercy of Nang and all the other patriots in the country. We just picked the wrong side." He tilted his head to the side as his life slowly left him.

He opened his eyes and turned back toward the major. "What you still don't know major is that you have not yet faced your most formidable enemy. All the civilians in Burma want you dead. Yes, I apologize for tricking you into killing our enemy who would have taken their homes back from us. But what would you have done under the same circumstance? We had stolen the Japanese weapons that you freed up for us, but we had no training or experience in their use. So now you are the villains, the ones who killed the innocent villagers who were returning home from their wartime stay in Yunnan. Better you than me.

"In fact, we would never have attacked you today if we hadn't heard about this meadow; a perfect spot for an ambush. Only you found out about our plans and ambushed us. Wait a minute---" He tried to raise up and look around, but the major held him down.

Duwa fell back and stared up at the sky and his eyes slowly closed. He was dead.

THIRTY-FOUR

"What was the butcher's toll?" This was an old saying from the days of the Royal Navy, also used by the Union Army's General Grant. The major was asking the sergeant major.

"Well sir. Private Gilbert was killed when a bullet passed through his neck, splitting his artery. Four others were injured by gun shot wounds but none too seriously. But there are more serious problems Sir. At least a dozen men have come down with jungle rot and can barely walk. They limp badly. And several men have contracted what appears to be malaria, and they all have high fever. They are all too proud to tell you sir, but you need to know."

"Yes, thank you sergeant. But that is strange. Jungle rot, or trench foot as it is often called, usually results from low temperature, something below 60 degrees. The first history of the problem comes to us from Napoleon's army returning from the Moscow winter in 1812. We haven't seen temperatures like that, have we sergeant?"

"We have Sir. At night some of the men kept their boots on when sleeping and apparently the temperature fell below 60 when we were high up on the mountain."

"All right sergeant. Tell the men to take their boots off and clean their feet when we reach a stream. Cleanliness is the most important way to protect against jungle rot. Also tell the men to bury the Japanese weapons with the bodies so that they don't fall into the hands of other guerillas."

The major and I were watching the men dig graves for the civilians they had killed. All their enemies had eventually succumbed in spite of the efforts of the men to save those who were only wounded. We were staring into the jungle trying to figure out how we got into this.

"Phil, there is something very strange going on here. I hate to be the conspiracy theorist in all of this, but I see Nang's hand everywhere I turn. I am haunted by what Duwa was trying to tell us when he died. There was something he said 'We heard about this meadow,' or something like that. When Nang told us about it she said that, 'they had discovered the meadow.'"

"My conspirator brain is confused. Let's review the meadow for a moment. If she were trying to do us in, what would be the best way? The best way would be for us to gather at the rear of Duwa's people ready to attack, and then her force would deploy behind and descend on us from our rear. She would know that we would be deployed away, facing Duwa's group and paying no attention to what was behind us. What could be more advantageous to a force that was trying to wipe us out? "Phil, I think that your decision to spread Sergeant O'Rourke and his six men behind us may have saved our butts. When she saw them, she decided that surprise was not possible and she fell back."

The major was getting into the conspiracy theory now. "Their spy in the Duwa camp could have stood up and said that there was a meadow up ahead that would provide the perfect spot for an ambush, and they took it from there. That may have been what Duwa was trying to tell us when he died."

THIRTY-FIVE

The two of us stared down at the jungle floor trying to piece together what had happened when we heard the familiar voice of Nang striding through the underbrush toward them. "Hi guys. What are you up to?" The two of us looked at each other then at her with badly concealed anger.

Looking away, I finally responded bitterly "We have been reviewing the events of the day and trying to decide to what we owed our good fortune," I said with unrestrained sarcasm.

"It looks to me like you did pretty well. I will, however, take credit for my part in your success and accept your gratitude," she said as she glared at us. "You Americans owe me." We again stared at each other in amazement. "However, I do have to comment on your suspicion of me by posting a guard in the rear of your troops. What were you concerned about?"

The two of us were having difficulty talking to her. "That is a standard military procedure in hostile territory, to post guards to prevent surprise enemy attacks from our flank," the major responded with some concern. "By the way, how did you know that we had set up a scouting patrol in our rear?" He glared at her with suspicion.

She had recovered her composure. "We know everything that goes on in our jungle. Are you getting more accepting of the need to kill civilians, Major?" Nang asked.

"No, we are not!" He almost shouted. The major was becoming more convinced that I was on to something with my conspiracy theory.

The men had finished their grizzly work and were packing up ready to move out. They looked haggard and angry. "How come we are always burying women and children?" Corporal Langston asked.

Lieutenant Schultz shrugged and took the lead motioning the men to follow. "I know of a really good spot to camp a couple of miles ahead," Nang said as she walked off following the troop. The two of us brought up the rear kicking the now dusty trail with disgust. After a couple of hours of walking through the jungle, we reached the spot Nang had talked about. "Yes, this is a good place to camp," she said. The major motioned to the lieutenant to pull off the trail. "Nang, don't go away." He was more composed, but not much. "I want to talk with you some more".

"Sure major. Whatever you say." They each sat on separate logs.

Nang sat facing the two of us with her Japanese rifle resting across her knees. She looked too comfortable and too at home with a weapon in her hands.

"Okay Nang, where do we stand?" Phil started by taking out his handkerchief and wiping his forehead in the heat. It seemed to him that he was perspiring too much for the temperature. "We are running low on food, ammunition and medicine. Our men are sick with dysentery, malaria, trench foot, and some are wounded. How far do we have to go to get to our lines?" I was convinced that he told her too much.

"I will tell you major. Come over here with me." The three of us got up and walked over to the edge of the clearing. "Do you see that mountain ridge?" she asked pointing to the northwest.

We squinted into the setting sun putting our hands up to shield our eyes. "Yes, and it's tall," I responded. "In fact, it looks to be several hundred feet tall, maybe a thousand feet."

"Yes. It is a tall mountain, and steep from this side. But it is your last barrier before getting home. The trail winds up this side to the top over there and then down into the Irrawaddi River Valley on the other side. If you turn slightly to your right when you get into the valley, the trail will take you to the Ledo Road, and from there it is a short walk into Myitkyina. You are almost there gentlemen."

We squinted into the sun and thought we could just make out a trail snaking up the side of the mountain. We turned and walked back to our campsite.

"You are not telling us what we want to know," I finally said when we had sat down again.

Nang smiled and responded, "Ah yes. You want to know about the remaining Burmese guerillas in this area and if they will attack you before you get home. Well, I have been talking with them for the past few days, trying to convince them that you are not their enemy. It has not been easy, but I think I have convinced them to let you get home without being attacked.

"In fact, I have convinced my people to bring you some of our food to share. They will be here in an hour or so. This should help with your outbreak of scurvy. It's not much because we don't have much. But the civilians of this forest are willing to help their friends, the Americans." We both glanced at each other.

"That's very kind of you, Nang. I am particularly happy because we are not much of a fighting force any more, and an attack, even by civilians, would be bloody." I wished Phil would shut up. The major pulled out his handkerchief and wiped his sweating forehead again.

"I will head out along the trail, meet them and urge them to hurry. I can see that your men need food badly." Nang rose off the log she was sitting on, threw the rifle over her shoulder, turned and walked off to the west.

THIRTY-SIX

Phil and I shared what was left of the fresh vegetables and rice that Nang's people had brought us after our troops had eaten the biggest portion. We felt better having finally eaten properly, but we were both concerned with what lay ahead of us. Our men were sick and some were wounded. Some were being carried on bamboo stretchers by men who were not in much better shape than their buddies on the stretchers. Neither of us knew how to begin the conversation.

"Damn, that woman knows how to confuse us. Was she giving us good news, or was she telling us that we faced a hell of a big battle coming up on that ridge over there?" I finally opened up the exchange that we both knew was coming.

"I don't know either, my friend. But we've got to assume the worst and prepare for it. Son of a bitch! Look at that trail. It goes straight up the side of that mountain. Anybody with a few guns sitting on top of that ridge could rain fire down on us, and there is nothing we could do to protect ourselves. I am concerned and fed up with this country!"

"Yah, and I don't believe for a minute that she is trying to save us. She will eventually do what she thinks is best for her and her goddamn people."

"Ray, let's get our scout in here and see what he has to say." The major was wiping his face again.

"Good idea." I jumped up and yelled instructions to the sergeant major who was setting up his camp a few yards away.

"Yes, Sir," the scout came running up.

"Do you see that steep ridge over there?" the major asked

"Yes Sir."

"We have got to cross it on that trail you see to get home. At least that's what Nang tells us. I would like you to scout around over there to the left and see if there is an alternate route, or if you think we can get over it without being massacred."

The scout jumped up. "I will return shortly major." "Ray, I thought that when we hung the colonel the war was over. But it was just getting started."

"I know. Sometimes in war you don't know who your enemy is. He seems to change from day to day."

"When we marched up this trail, the Burmese civilians were our friends, helping us with food and local intelligence. Then, on the way home, we listened to bad intelligence and mistakenly killed locals in hopes of getting back alive."

"And all we did was dig ourselves deeper and deeper into a hole," the major responded. "Do you remember on our trip up here if we passed over that ridge?"

"I was just thinking about that, Phil. I seem to remember that the walk up the other side was much more shallow, not so steep. But remember when we reached the top, we looked down at the steep trail on this side and we took another way, another trail or something. Do you recall?"

"Ah yes, we turned south and walked along the ridge for a short distance. The trail soon turned into a densely overgrown area that allowed us to drop down off the mountain gradually in heavy jungle, giving us lots of cover. Hum, I wonder if we could find that path from this side."

"Let's think this through and see what we can come up with. We'll talk more in the morning."

We both retreated to our hammocks and prepared to crawl in. But before I undressed, I recalled a question I wanted to ask my friend, and I walked back over to Phil's hammock. When I arrived, I could hear the major's teeth chattering and see the hammock shaking as he lay curled up with his blanket wrapped around him in the heat of the evening.

I stood there a minute, then turned and walked away.

My God, he has malaria, I thought.

THIRTY-SEVEN

"Alright men. Let's gather 'round and listen up." The major felt a little better this morning and did not want his men to know how sick he really was. He had taken a couple of quinine tablets after swearing the medic to secrecy on the threat of having his throat cut.

"We may or may not be in for a big fight. I don't know for sure. But you all see that mountain up ahead. We have to walk over it to get home, and I have reason to believe that there are enemies all around us. If there are, they will certainly attack us as we climb up that mountain toward the ridge. If we can get over that ridge, we have an easy walk home, only a few miles beyond. The question we face is how do we get over that ridge without being attacked?" The men noticed that sweat was forming on his brow, and it was still early morning. He turned toward me in hopes I would continue the conversation.

I did. "If our concerns are justified, our enemy will be strung out along that ridge with their weapons pointing down at us awaiting our arrival. By the time we reach the top, we will be exhausted and hardly ready for a fight." No one was happy with what they heard.

"We have all got to be prepared for the fight of our lives. Every man, even the sick and wounded, must be prepared to fire his weapon. There is no sick call today." The men looked at each other.

"Who is our enemy, captain?" a soldier from the rear asked the question that was on everyone's mind.

"I have to be honest with you men. I am not sure," the major responded to him. "Nang has told us that there is a large group of Burmese civilians living in this area who think we are trying to take over their country like the Japanese and English did before us. They are well armed with stolen Japanese and English weapons, and they know how to use them. She has been trying to convince them that we are not their enemy, but she is not sure if they believe her. We may be worried in vain, but we must be prepared."

After a short pause, I continued, "At the foot of the mountain, just a couple of miles ahead, our scout tells us that the trail splits and a small, well-hidden fork takes off to the left. He thinks that this is the one we took down the mountain when we came the other way a few weeks ago." The major took over the conversation again as I must have looked at him with concern. "The fork is still in the jungle so we will not be exposed to the ridge yet, Lieutenant Schultz." "Sir?"

"You will lead the stretcher and wounded group ahead, and yes, you will be our bait as you were before. But this time, I want you to stop just as you become exposed but are not yet in the sunlight or within range of their guns. I want the enemy, if he is up there, to see you and think that you have stopped to care for the wounded.

"Fuss over the stretchers and look like you have stopped to change bandages or something that looks real. In the meantime, the rest of us will work our way along the jungle trail to our left and attack their right flank on the ridge while they are watching you down here. Does that make sense to everybody?"

"Yes Sir."

"And lieutenant. When you hear firing, you can assume that the enemy is concentrating on us from their flank, so move out along the trail and up the hill as fast as you can with the stretchers and wounded. I want the enemy to be faced with attack from two sides. Also, you must leave the remaining mules down here. Cut them loose and let them roam free. That's the least we can do for them. They can't get up that trail as fast as we need to move."

The lieutenant nodded wondering what kind of a fighting force his group of sick soldiers would be.

The major looked at me. "Have I left anything out Ray?"

I think that's it Phil," I replied with more confidence than I felt.

THIRTY-EIGHT

"How do you hack through this jungle and do it quietly?" The men were working their way up the south trail as fast and quietly as they could. Everyone was sweating and puffing and swearing with each step. Apparently, no one had been along this trail since we had come down the mountain a few weeks before, and the undergrowth had begun to reclaim it.

The men thought they could see cobras, tigers, pythons and terrorists behind each bush. Because they had been given strict orders not to fire their weapons unless ordered, or if their life depended on it, they kept their safeties on. The trail was much longer than we remembered, probably because we were walking up hill this time.

Soon the trail began to level off, and we came to the edge of a clearing on top of the ridge. The major raised his hand, and the column came to a stop. The men gratefully dropped down to rest. Phil and I crouched down and then moved out into the clearing to look over the terrain.

The top of the mountain had leveled off and become a mesa covered with rocks of all sizes but with little vegetation. The trail weaved around the rock formations along the ridge to the north. The two of us could see the trail break over the summit a few hundreds yards ahead where it joined the main trail we were on earlier. It headed to the northwest and dropped down into the Irrawaddi Valley below.

"Ray, I see no sign of an enemy, nor any reason to be worried. What do you think?"

I cautiously looked around and walked over to the eastern ridge and looked down toward the jungle we had left a short time ago. I could see Lieutenant Schultz and the stretchers resting at the edge of the clearing. I walked back to the major now standing upright.

"No, Phil. I see nothing that looks suspicious," I reported. We both looked back at our men, now completely exhausted and resting in the shade. Phil thought he would give them a little more rest before striking out across the open mesa.

Soon he said in a loud whisper, "Okay men, let's continue on, but be careful, and stay alert." The men slowly rose from their rest and began walking out into the sunlight weaving through the boulder-covered landscape. The major, leading the column, looked back and saw that all of his men were now out in the open following him along the trail. "This is the moment of truth," he said to me. "If we are going to get it, it will be----"

The sound was like nothing we had ever heard before. Dozens of rifles and sub machine guns opened up on us at once. Bullets whistled around our heads, bouncing off the boulders and some hitting their targets before the troops could drop to the ground. Many others were hit trying to crawl to safety before they could reach the cover of the boulders.

Fortunately, Phil and I were close enough to a large boulder that we were able to crawl behind it, as bullets were ricocheting off its surface. Those who reached the safety of a large enough boulder to shield them from incoming rounds took their weapons off their shoulders, released the safeties and began to return fire. Unfortunately, the enemy troops were well hidden behind boulders of their own and were not easily seen.

The major looked back at his men. "My God Ray. At least half of our troops are lying on the ground, dead or wounded." I didn't respond. There was nothing to add. I had removed the safety and was firing my M-1 carbine in rapid sequence, aiming at anything that moved. The major returned his concentration to the flash of weapons raining down on our men from boulders less than hundred yards away.

The enemy was slightly higher than we, but not as much above us as they would have been had the column come up the main trail. Phil could have switched his beloved Thompson to automatic fire, but he would soon be out of ammunition, so he kept in semi-automatic, firing one bullet at a time.

"Look Ray, they are moving toward us, one boulder after the next. Maybe we have a chance to pick a few off."

The firing became more intense as the enemy forces ran from boulder to boulder, heading toward us and firing continuously. Our men had settled down a bit and were waiting for a good shot to pick off a charging enemy. Even the major had brought down several. The enemy troops were not good shots, but they were good enough. The major could hear the cries of his soldiers as they were hit.

The major slammed another magazine in his sub machine gun to replace the empty one he threw on the ground. He turned back toward the onrushing enemy and fired as rapidly as he could.

Suddenly the enemy's firing stopped, and the two of us looked at each other and wondered why. There was no obvious reason. They were all hidden behind boulders again, but this time much closer, maybe thirty yards. We both crouched, one on each side of a large protective boulder. We carefully stuck our heads out to see what was going on. It was eerily calm. The major looked back over his men and saw many more down. Then it started again! This time accompanied by screaming like we had never heard before.

We both thought that it was the Banzai scream used by the Japanese soldiers when they made their last charge. But this was a higher pitch, like maybe it was----

Now they came at us all at once, including a group from their right flank that I had to deal with. But some one was charging directly at Major Jenkins, and he leveled his weapon ready to bring down the charging enemy. It seemed to all of us like he had an easy shot.

Then he saw it. This person charging at him was a woman, a woman with a small child strapped to her back. She was firing a Japanese rifle at him, cocking the bolt action that threw another round in the chamber, and firing again. She did all this while charging straight at the major, carrying her child.

I saw Phil's jaw drop as he peered out across his barrel, but he was unable to pull the trigger. He saw out of the corner of his eye that all of the "troops" charging his men were all women and young girls, with an occasional teen age boy thrown in. His antagonist fired another round past his ear. He still couldn't bring himself to pull the trigger. She cocked her rifle again and was now only a few feet away.

"For Christ sake, major, pull the trigger," he heard one of his nearby soldiers shout at him, but he couldn't.

Then he felt a burning sensation in his left rib cage below his shoulder just as he saw the soldier who had been yelling at him bring down the charging woman and her baby. That was all he remembered as he slumped to the ground and lost consciousness.

Exposing myself to the relentless fire, I reached over to grab him and set him upright behind the boulder that had protected us. I finally dragged him to a safe position then turned to continue firing, but before I could get off another round, I felt cold steel pressing against the back of my head. It was immediately obvious what was pressing against my head. I recognized it as the barrel of a

"Tell your men to stop firing and drop their weapons immediately captain." I recognized Nang's voice as I reluctantly shouted at the men to surrender. They all dropped their weapons and raised their hands. The shooting stopped, and only groans from the wounded could be heard.

THIRTY-NINE

The dead and wounded men and women had been dragged and carried into a small grove of trees to get them out the blazing sun. The medic was attending to the major, trying to stop his bleeding as he lay on the ground in the shade. The wounded were all being helped as well as possible in this hot, remote part of Burma.

"How did you know we would be coming up the side trail rather than the main trail?" I finally asked.

"That was too damn easy captain. No experienced soldier would expose his men to that route. We knew about this jungle trail and assumed you would know about it too. The ruse that Lieutenant Schultz tried to pull off was amusing, but not convincing. When he heard the firing, we saw him carry his wounded back into the jungle. We will get him when we finish with you.

"Unfortunately, captain, you were outsmarted by a group of rice-growing children-rearing Burmese women and a few old men who knew enough about this jungle to follow and ambush your highly trained soldiers. I believe you call yourselves Merrill's Marauders!

"But don't worry you poor bastard, I won't tell anybody what happened to you. We will let your superior officers believe that you died fighting Japanese soldiers. We won't torture you; we only do that to the Japanese who raped our country."

"But why you Nang? We thought you were our friend. We fed and clothed you and let you do your will with our prisoners. Why in the hell have you turned against us?" I shouted.

"Well, technically, I never turned against you. I was never really 'for' you Americans. Actually, if you remember back, Colonel Maruyama was right when he warned you that I was not to be trusted. Oh yes, I liked you all, but I couldn't allow my personal feelings to keep me from killing you when the time was right. You also were very useful in killing my enemies along the way. All we had to do was sit back and cheer you along. It is funny how you American soldiers will believe anything a woman tells you.

"The major's argument with the colonel about the evils of killing civilians was very interesting. Civilians are not in the front lines, at least not until all the men are killed. Although you are professional fighters, we knew that we had the advantage when you saw that we were women and children. Your major was not the only one of your men who refused to pull the trigger as we charged.

"Don't forget, in the wars of the future, the difference between soldiers and the civilians they are fighting will sometimes be indistinguishable. As the colonel told you, if you become the leader of your country, don't ever take your people to war without accepting the fact that you are going to kill civilians, lots of them. 'We only intend to kill soldiers and will not harm women and children' is a fool's tale intended only to lure a country into a war that it should not be fighting."

She felt guilty about advising him never to lead his country into future wars knowing that he would not live through the day. "Will your 'moral' country ever learn that lesson? Not likely.

"So now you and your major must die, captain. I will make it as quick and painless as possible." She cocked the hammer back on her .45 and raised it slowly toward his head as the other women selected a target from the sitting Americans and did the same. Then the firing started again.

I had my eyes closed, in hopes that the pain of death would not be too great. But I strangely felt no pain, no blood streaming down my fore head. So I opened one eye and then the other in time to see Nang come crashing to the ground with blood spurting out of her mouth and a massive wound through the top of her head.

I looked around to see some women falling mortally wounded and others trying to run away. They weren't firing their guns. I looked behind me in the direction in which the firing was originating. I was surprised to see maybe a dozen or more wounded Americans following Lieutenant Schultz all running toward us and firing their weapons into the crowd of Burmese women and men. In a few seconds, it was all over; the enemy was on the ground screaming and dying.

I finally got my composure and sense of humor back. "Welcome lieutenant! And what took you so long?"

The lieutenant walked up to Nang with a smile on his dirt and sweat covered face. Looking down at her bloody body, he said, "You made two mistakes Nang. You failed to post a lookout to watch the main trail coming up the mountain, and you assumed that I was a coward and was running away with the wounded under my care.

"No American soldier, no matter how badly wounded, would leave his unit to be massacred without trying to help. But then, that's the way we Merrill's Marauders are trained." He finished with considerable sarcasm in his voice.

Nang started to say something, but her eyes slowly closed as death took over before anything came out. I reached over and took the bowie knife I had given her from her scarf and slipped the scabbard back into my belt. It felt good to have my grandfather's knife back where it belonged.

"Okay, lets get these bodies covered up as best as we can," I finally said to no one in particular.

FORTY

The men who were not wounded had built a bamboo stretcher for the major; the few able bodied men left grabbed a corner of a stretcher and lifted one or more weapons onto their shoulders. "Okay Lieutenant Schultz, you have the lead. Take us home now and don't spare the horsepower," I shouted to our now second in command.

"Yes Sir!"

At least it was downhill now toward the Irrawaddi. We could see the magnificent river through the trees. As the men struggled down the hill, some barely able to walk, they could see rice patties in the distance with women bent over working in the fields. It was getting dark as I shouted, "Find us a place to spend the night lieutenant." The lieutenant turned around and waved in acknowledgement. We soon crossed a small creek with a forest opening next to it. We pulled off and set up camp.

"Hopefully this will be our last night in this place captain," the medic said as he bent down over the major.

"I hope so too corporal. Do you have any quinine left for the major?" I bent over to hear his labored breathing.

"No Sir, I gave out all I had yesterday."

I certainly knew that my old friend would have wanted it that way. "Do we have any food left?"

"We were able to salvage some from our enemies up on the ridge. I will fix you some rice and pork."

"I would appreciate that corporal. God, I hope I never see rice again."

After I ate, I sat down next to Phil and held his hand, took his pulse and listened to his breathing. "Hang on Phil, we will be home tomorrow. I wish we had some blood for you. I would gladly give you mine, but it is the wrong type and Corporal Dixon says that there are too many germs in this jungle to risk a transfusion here." Did my friend hear me? The major gave no response.

We were up early, eating the last of our food and preparing to get back on the trail so that we could continue heading for home. One wounded soldier had died in the middle of the night. Now that I was in charge, I read his eulogy over the shallow grave with its homemade cross-planted at his head.

The Burmese scout had been killed in the fight on the ridge, so we were feeling our way by compass, wherever the trail took us. At least we were headed toward the river and civilization. "Okay, lieutenant, take us home," I ordered. The lieutenant waved to me in response from the head of the column.

The jungle began to thin out, and we could see the mountains in the distance and what appeared to be a road on the side of one hill.

From my spot in the rear of the column, walking next to the major being carried in a stretcher, I could see that the lieutenant had spotted the road, too, and had turned slightly to head toward it. Good man, Lieutenant Schultz. I have got to remember to give him a promotion when we get back.

The sun was intense and getting hotter now that the jungle was behind us. As we passed near by rice patties, women with children strapped to their backs looked up and stared at us without showing emotion. It occurred to me that they had probably been doing this for tens of thousands of years, watching invading armies come and go. Their men went off to war and the women were left to defend their farms and families. We all stopped and stared at a small group of women standing about a hundred yards away and looking at us.

The female of the species is more deadly than the male. I had forgotten the entire poem, but I remembered it had said something about women facing death every time they gave birth. Of course, males thought it was no big deal.

I put my head down and hurried to catch up with the end of the column. Kipling knew what he was talking about. After all, he had spent a big part of his life living here in Burma.

Walking across the Irrawaddi flood plain was not easy. The heat was becoming more intense every minute. The men thought it was bad enough walking through the jungle mud. They were convinced now that this was even worse. It was probably harder because they were carrying the wounded and sick on stretchers, some draped across their backs. The only thing that gave them hope was the dirt road they could see running along the mountain ahead. As we approached, it seemed like a mirage. "It won't be long now, unless, of course, it is a mirage," I said to the sergeant.

We came to a slight rise, which allowed us to see farther ahead. "Look captain. There is the road, and it's not far ahead."

"Yes corporal, I see it too." Then I noticed something even more striking; in the distance a long line of trucks was coming down the road. I couldn't believe my eyes. "Lieutenant," I suddenly shouted.

"Run up ahead get on that road and stop those trucks. Stop them if you have to lie in front of them until we can get there."

Lieutenant Schultz turned, dropped his carbine, and sprinted off toward the road at full speed. He was in the best shape of any of his soldiers, I thought, although that wasn't saying much Our men slowly continued walking and crawling toward the road praying the lieutenant would get there before the trucks arrived. "Look captain," the sergeant major was in the lead now although severely wounded himself. "There is a whole string of deuce and a halves." We could see the lieutenant getting closer to the road. I realized that I hadn't heard that phrase used to describe the workhorse two-and-a-half-ton army trucks in several years.

The lieutenant, now completely out of breath, scampered up the final incline onto the road as the lead truck came around the bend. Unable to stand, he waved both hands frantically from a kneeling position. The lead truck began to let out a squeal as the driver applied the brakes, finally coming to a stop a few feet in front of Lieutenant Schultz.

The driver slammed on the parking brake and he and his "shotgun" both opened their doors, jumped to the roadway and ran up to the lieutenant, now lying flat in the dusty road. They both started talking at once, while helping him to sit up. Trucks and jeeps that were coming up from behind ground to a halt, and men jumped out and ran up to see what was going on.

"If you guys will stop asking a bunch of stupid questions, I'll tell you who the hell we are." He pointed out over the plain toward the remainder of our unit walking as fast as we could toward them.

The major in charge of the convoy now ran up and pushed his men aside in time to see the lieutenant pointing out across the open country to the south east. The major looked up and, putting his hand over his eyes, could make out what looked like a band of rag-tag frontiersmen barley able to walk. Some were in wornout uniforms, some were in underwear. They were about three hundred yards away. Many were carrying stretchers; some were helping their friends to walk, all limping toward freedom.

"My God," Major Jones exclaimed. "Who are you?" He looked back at the lieutenant.

"We are the last of Merrill's Marauders, the 5307th,

The major took his hand down from his forehead and turned to the rear of his truck column. He cupped his hands around his mouth and shouted, "Sergeant, take all the men we can spare, run down and help those poor bastards get up here."

"Lieutenant, are you okay?" he asked looking down at the sitting, worn out soldier.

"I am mostly tired, Sir. I don't think I can walk much further."

"You won't have to lieutenant. Our trucks are mostly empty, and I think we can fit you all in. This is the Ledo Road, recently renamed the Stillwell Road, as you may know. Since the war ended we have been bringing our trucks back to India from Yunnan. First, we go through Myitkyina, just a few miles down the road where we have a military hospital. But let's get you all on board and head for home."

He turned to the sergeant who was leading the convoy. "When you get loaded sergeant, step on it."

The convoy commander turned to watch his men take over carrying the stretchers and helping the walking wounded climb up the last few feet they would have to walk to safety. I was in the lead. I saluted the major and smiled "Good afternoon, Sir."

The major returned the salute, and looked at me in horror. "My God, what have you guys been through?"

Just then, four of the convoy men walked up carrying Major Jenkins' stretcher and set it in the dust in front of them. "This is our commanding officer, Major Jenkins, Sir." The convoy commander looked down as a tear began to form in his eyes. "He was wounded in a fire fight yesterday," I said, and he has malaria."

He didn't look like there was much life left in him, but he was breathing. The convoy's medic had arrived and reached into his pouch and pulled out a few quinine pills, reached down, held the major's head and gave him water from his canteen to get the pills down. Major Jenkins was apparently unconscious but was able to swallow the pills.

The medic ripped open the major's shirt to expose his chest wound. He and the others standing around gasped. Without saying anything, the medic tore off the bloody bandage, then reached back into his pouch and pulled out sulfa powder and sprinkled it over his chest. He then reached in and pulled out a clean bandage and applied it over the wound. Men standing around watching put their hands over their mouths and turned to walk away before they threw up. The convoy commander pulled out his handkerchief and wiped his eyes.

"Captain, you and the major will ride in the first truck. Corporal Hansen, you will ride with them, and please try to keep the major alive until we reach the hospital in Myitkyina."

"Get those men loaded up and let's get the hell out of here."

FORTY-ONE

It was a bumpy ride. The driver was obeying his major's orders as he roared down the dirt road toward the hospital at top speed. Major Jenkins was lying in his stretcher in the center of the truck's bed. I was sitting on the bench next to him and the medic was sitting on the bench across from me. I was holding my friend's hand firmly as the medic cleaned the wound and put the bandage back on his chest. Then he wiped the sweat from his forehead.

"Hang on Phil. We are almost there," I said.

Then a miracle happened. The major awoke from his unconscious state for the first time since he was shot. He blinked at me. "Hello Ray. Where the hell are we?"

I was able to choke back a gasp. "Hi Phil. Stay down. We are in a deuce and a half taking you to the hospital at Myitkyina, at top speed I might add," as we bumped along.

The major looked around the truck and nodded an acknowledgement to the corporal, seeing the red cross on his armband. "I don't feel too good, Ray." The corporal and I looked at each other as the major fell back into unconsciousness.

After a few minutes, Phil awoke again. "My memory has left me Ray, but it seems like we have been in some pretty good fights."

"Yes we were Phil, and we won everyone of them." The major seemed to hold my hand even tighter.

"Yes, I remember now. They were tough battles, but our boys killed them all, didn't they?"

"Yes they did, Phil."

After a while, the major opened his eyes wide and raised up to look at me. "But we never killed any civilians did we Ray? I couldn't live with myself if I thought I had killed any civilians." He had become delirious.

I nodded, "No Phil, we didn't kill any civilians." I knew that God would forgive me for my little lie.

The major leaned back on his stretcher happy with my response.

After a few minutes with his eyes closed, he opened them and looked back at me. "You remember, Ray, the Japanese colonel, whose name I have forgotten, tried to convince me that it was okay, in fact necessary, to kill civilians to win a war. That was about the dumbest thing I ever heard. I think that it was more of a rationalization on his part for what the Japanese did in this war. Do you remember the burned out villages we passed through on our way to get him? But we finally got him, didn't we Ray?"

The major was talking fast now, not waiting for an answer. It was as if he had lots to say and little time to say it in.

"Just because the war had ended didn't mean that we were going to let that son of a bitch get away, did it Ray? I'll bet that all the villagers in that jungle were happy that we got him. They all helped us get home, didn't they?"

I nodded slowly without saying anything.

"They helped us get home, in spite of the troops we had to fight. By the way, don't forget to give Sergeant Hashimoto his promotion to lieutenant when we get home. He is a brave man."

The corporal kept pouring water from his canteen on his towel and wiping the major's forehead.

"War is terrible isn't it Ray? We think we know who our enemy is, and then he changes---" His words trailed off as if he were trying to remember something.

"You know Ray. I believe that no president, or leader of any country, should declare war on anyone unless he has been to war himself. Until he has looked someone in the eye and pulled the trigger that ends his life. And I don't mean being in the Navy or Air Corps.

They never see the results of their damage. They go home each evening to the officer's club, have a drink and go to sleep in their warm beds." No, all future presidents should be infantrymen who carry death on their shoulders and have to decide who to kill.

"Whoever pulls the trigger or pushes the button that kills has got to come face to face with the results of his decisions. I suspect that that will end wars forever."

The major closed his eyes and fell back unconscious. I held onto his hand tightly.

The major awoke again and looked up at me. "How many enemy troops did we kill altogether, Ray? Do you know?"

"But you and I were together for over three years, weren't we? We must have killed hundreds, would you say?"

"Well, war is not for the faint at heart, nor for women, is it Ray?"

We could hear people talking along the road now as the truck slowed to turn into the city and toward the hospital.

The major opened his eyes again and looked up at me. "I don't know if I am going to make it Ray, but if I don't please tell my wife and daughters that I love them, and that I am happy they will never have to go to war----."

His head fell back and his eyes closed as the truck screeched to a halt in front of the emergency entrance. The corporal grabbed the major's wrist to feel for pulse and put his other hand on his neck. He looked up at me and shook his head.

The back gate opened and four soldiers grabbed the stretcher and pulled it out of the truck and set it on the ground. The leading sergeant looked down at Major Jenkins and then back at me.

"So am I sergeant. So am I." I put my head in both hands and sobbed uncontrollably as they carried off my best friend's lifeless body.

FORTY-TWO

"Dad, can I talk to you for a minute?"

"Sure Mark. Let me get seated and then we can talk," I responded to my son as I walked out of the kitchen with a drink in my hand. My son was at the age where relating to me did not happen very often. He was near graduation from high school and talking to his father occurred only when necessary. I settled into my chair and smiled. "What's up?"

"Well dad, a soldier came to our school today and talked to us about joining the Marine Corps after graduation instead of getting drafted into the infantry. He had a number of stripes on his arms and said that he was a recruiter for the Corps. The school had set up a meeting for the senior boys so that he could present the Marine Corp's argument for joining up." I took a sip and scowled. "So what did he say?"

"Well he talked about the value of joining a unit that would give you pride and self confidence, as if being drafted into the Army was second best. With the war going on, he said we would all be going to Vietnam one way or another. So why not join the very best?"

"So what is it you want to know, son?

"It is not so much which unit to join. The question is why would anyone want to go to war in the first place?"

"No one ever wants to go to war, Mark. It is only something that we must do periodically to protect our country and our way of life." The room was silent as we looked at each other.

"That's what I don't fully understand Dad. This war seems to have nothing to do with protecting our freedom. People who are struggling to throw out foreigners from their country are fighting it in a far-off jungle in South East Asia. They have been doing this for dozens, maybe hundreds of years."

I smiled slightly hearing my son share some of the same thoughts I had expressed in Burma in the 1940's.

"You have told me stories of your own fighting experiences during World Was II and the intensity with which the Burmese civilians fought to rid their country of the dreaded foreign armies. How is this war different?"

I had to think back over the stories I had told my son through the years about how the desire for freedom had caused poorly trained and inadequately armed civilians to do things that were not militarily smart and could not possibly result in victory. I reviewed in my mind the frantic charges and fanatic do-or-die efforts of the Burmese women and children in their hope for independence. But this war was different.

"You don't understand son. These enemy forces are Communists who will expand their influence and control if they prevail. Soon we will have to fight them on the California shores." I admit that I wasn't very convincing, even to myself. The room fell silent again as we both squirmed in our seats.

"Anyway, there is a war on, and you are going to have to serve your country in one form or another." I was surprised at the look on my son's face.

"I don't know dad. It seems to me that in a country based on freedom, we all have the responsibility to make an informed decision when it comes to how we want to spend our lives. In your war, the choice was easy. Our country was being threatened with invasion and annihilation. The problem is not that my life will be in danger in Vietnam, but that I will be expected to kill other people who are only fighting for their freedom.

"You say that if they win, they will soon be on our west coast, but that doesn't make sense either Dad. Have you seen them? They are peasants dressed in pajamas and hardly capable of attacking another country even if they wanted to." I started to answer but couldn't think of a rebuttal.

"I know that you are dedicated to the defense of our country Dad and spent four years of your life doing so. But I often wonder, how much did your efforts contribute to our victory? Suppose you and your major friend, what was his name, Phil, had just sat down and had a beer with your Japanese colonel instead of hanging him from a tree? Would that have made a big difference in the lives we lead today? Remember the doctors' motto, 'First, do no harm.' Shouldn't that be the motto of all of civilization? How can we justify travelling eight thousand miles, mass killing civilians, and then coming back to our sedentary lives here in the states? Can you give me just one reason why I should do that?"

"Well son, if you don't, you will probably end up in a federal prison for a couple of years. That should be enough to persuade you."

"But isn't that a flimsy reason for killing innocent people who are just trying to live their own lives without foreign domination? Isn't that the reason we fought to rid ourselves of the British government in the eighteenth century? I don't get it dad. You are not giving me answers that make sense."

I had to think fast. My son was beginning to sound like Colonel Maruyama in Burma. "The President has determined that it is in our country's best interest to help our South Vietnamese allies to rid their country of their aggressors from the north. To an old Army man like your father, that alone is enough reason to go to war."

"Is it really dad? That's probably the worst reason you have given me so far."

I had to agree, but I wasn't going to admit it. It once was the only reason a person needed to join up, but not any more. I could remember when President Roosevelt put out the call for men to volunteer to serve their country and fight to the death if necessary, and it indeed cost my best friend his life. But those days seemed long gone, and maybe that was for the best. However, now I had to talk my son into staying out of jail and for what? To spend the rest of his life wondering why he had killed innocent Vietnamese civilians?

I remembered that my friend, Phil, had hesitated to pull the trigger for an instant when he realized that the attacking enemy was a group of women and children. His momentary indecision cost Phil his life. I had held Phil's hand as his life left him. Now my son had to make similar choices, only the alternatives were different. Spend two years in federal prison or march through the Southeast Asia jungle killing Vietnamese. What a choice life gives us.

"Maybe I can get you a deferment. I know several people on the draft board."

"No Dad. That's not an option. I don't want a deferment based on political influence. Yes, I know that there are sons of high-ranking officials and politicians who have made religious or moral claims that have gotten them out of service. But it seems to me that we shouldn't have to make excuses for not wanting to kill other human beings. What's wrong with that reasoning?"

I had to think for a while. "There is nothing wrong with that reasoning Mark. It is just that our President will put you in jail for using it. It is a simple choice; just be aware of the consequences of your decision."

Mark smiled. "Just think Dad. If everyone thought the way I do and refused to fight, there would be no more wars. Our country could spend that money on education, helping the poor and building a stronger country." I failed to see his logic.

"You know Mr. Boggs, the president of the bank in town. He served with you in Burma, didn't he?"

"He was in Burma, but not in our group."

"Well you know how fanatic he is about everyone serving in the military if their country needs them. He won't give you a bank account if he thinks you are a conscientious objector."

"Yes, I have heard that."

"Well anyway, he is an expert in jungle warfare from his World War II experience. What you probably don't know is that he received a letter from our government recently asking him to join up again and help the Army train new recruits how to fight in the jungle. And you know what he said? He wrote back and refused to go. He said that he had too much to do here in Santa Fe. Do you detect a little hypocrisy here?"

"Yes I do, Mark. But what does that have to do with your decision? He has served his country, and now it is your turn."

"Well for one thing, maybe we can look forward to not hearing him berate teenagers for not wanting to go to Vietnam and kill innocent people. But that is probably expecting too much."

I did not appreciate my son's humor.

"So what is next? When do you have to make a decision?"

"Not until after I graduate in June. After that, it's up to the draft board." I nodded and got up to mix myself another drink.

FORTY-THREE

I was staring down at the grass that covered this beautiful graveyard, wondering if I would ever be buried in such a beautiful place. I was happy that Lieutenant Schultz had survived the war. In fact, he stayed in the Army making it a career and finally retired as a brigadier general after serving bravely in Korea and in Vietnam. I would love to see him again, share the pictures I'm taking, and reminisce over the perilous times we spent together in this jungle. My thoughts strayed.

I often wondered if his time here in Burma helped him survive in the jungles of Vietnam twenty years later and just a few miles east of here. It's great that we still correspond after all these years, my mind wandered back. I stood up and walked over to Major Jenkins' gravesite and looked down. "We had some great times together Phil, and you were a top commanding officer. I learned how to kill and stay alive from you. You were a great friend and leader."

There were a few things we never did figure out though. Who was Nang and what was her real agenda? And who were those Burmese women who were trying to kill us? I guess we will never know, will we Phil?

Actually you may know now. It is just that I don't. I lie awake at night reliving the whole thing, wondering how we could have done it differently, but nothing ever comes to me. I think we did what we had to.

I reached into my inner coat pocket and slowly pulled out a beautiful leather scabbard covered with Spanish carvings obviously made by a master carver. With my other hand I pulled out the razor sharp bowie knife. I turned it over in my hand, admiring the blade that I hadn't used since 1945. I held it up so that the sun could reflect off it, and I could marvel at its beauty. How many men did I kill with this? I smiled without answering.

Without thinking, I gave it to a woman who was dedicated to killing us. What a mistake that was! Thank God I got it back, all because of Lieutenant, now General, Schultz. My grandfather would have killed me if I had come home without our family treasure.

After several minutes of turning it around in my hands, I returned it to its scabbard and slipped it back into my coat. I patted my chest covering the knife.

I stared out to the Irrawaddi from Phil's grave, thinking and reminiscing. Then it hit me. Wait a minute. There must be a World War II history museum or something like that in this town.

I looked down at Phil's grave for what I thought would be that last time. Got to go Phil. This is maybe the last time I see you. It's a long way from here to New Mexico, and I am getting too old for this traveling stuff. I will pass on your love to your family back home. I started to leave.

Then the thought struck me. No one will probably ever visit you again my friend. Who would want to travel 12,000 miles to see the grave of someone who they didn't know or couldn't remember? I looked around at the other sites. Someone had sat out flowers on the graves. I kicked myself for not doing that. A tear came to my eye as I walked to the road.

It took a while to get the taxi driver to understand where I wanted to go, and he didn't know if such a place existed. After several minutes of gesturing and trying Pigeon English, the driver finally smiled and nodded. He closed the door as the taxi sped off, and I again watched the river flow by.

What am I going to ask for? Does anyone around here speak English? I paid the driver and turned to look at a magnificent marble building with a long staircase leading to big carved mahogany doors. I started up.

The lady at the front desk understood enough English to know that I needed to see someone who could speak my language better than she did. After a short conversation on the phone, she smiled and motioned for me to sit down in the lobby. Someone would be with me shortly.

I sat there a while admiring the architecture when finally a well-dressed young man walked up with an outretched hand. "Hello, my name is Mr. Salai, and I understand that you have some questions for us in English. How can I help?"

"Yes, thank you," I introduced myself. "I was stationed here during much of World War II and have come back to visit the gravesites of some of my comrades. While here, I thought I would search out any history you might have of a Burmese woman we heard about during the war by the name of Nang. Unfortunately, I never knew her last name, so I'm not optimistic that you will know who I'm talking about or have any information about her."

"Here it is," he said as he dusted off the cover. "It isn't much of a best seller these days, but it was once very popular. Please sit over here and take as much time as you like to read it, but I can't let you take it out. It's our only copy. And please wear these plastic gloves to protect the pages."

I sat down at the table and carefully opened the cover. Written by someone by the name of Maung. That's interesting, I thought.

"By the way," Mr. Salai had returned. "Maung is not necessarily his given name. Burmese aren't given surnames at birth, and will often adopt one or change their name, as they grow older. Maung typically means that he is an author."

It was a typical biography translated into English and obviously written by someone who was very fond of the principal character. I thumbed through the first part quickly, the part that covered her exploits during the early part of the war which was of no immediate interest to me. It then described her attempt to kill the Japanese

Colonel Maruyama, which ended in an ambush, wiping out most of her unit. I had heard all of this from her.

But then it got more interesting. "Nang's terrorist unit was made up almost entirely of Burmese women and young girls!" I read. My God! I put the book down. Of course! It was her unit of guerillas that tried to kill us, and they were mostly women. I stared out the window reliving the battle on the ridge and the screaming women who charged down it shooting at us as they killed my best friend. Colonel Maruyama was right. She was a terrorist, a leader of a band of guerrilla women who were dedicated to ridding their country of all foreigners.

I lifted the book again and continued reading. My mouth soon dropped again. "Nang's husband was a man by the name of Duwa who led a group of villagers living in the northern jungle. He was killed in a skirmish against an unknown enemy shortly after the war ended.

"Duwa had shown sympathies for the invading Japanese, but when the war ended, he became more concerned with saving his followers from the anger of the local villagers. It was never determined who killed Duwa and his followers, but some said that there was an American Army unit in the area. However, this has never been confirmed."

"My God! We killed her husband!" I exclaimed loudly to no one in particular as I jumped up. No wonder she was mad at us. She was using her husband as a decoy when she alerted Phil the he would try to ambush us along the trail. She was planning a surprise attack from our rear when we would least expect it. Phil saved us by posting a guard to warn of such an attack from behind. Instead, we killed her husband and his villagers. Unbelievable! But now, it's all beginning to make sense.

Lost in thought, I looked up in time to see a Burmese man walking toward me. As I stared at him, I thought that he had some Anglo look in his face. "Hello. My name is Maung, and I am the author of the book you are reading. I am also the mayor of Myitkyina. Mr. Salai called me and told me that an American was reading my book and was very interested in my mother, Nang." He had a disarming smile that caused me to gasp. My mouth moved, but nothing came out.

"He says that you were in the Army here during the war and heard about my mother from other soldiers. You have not finished my book yet, but it has a very unsatisfactory ending. May I join you?" He sat down before I could answer.

"You see, I could never find out exactly how my mother was killed or who killed her. My book says all we know which is that she and her band of guerillas were killed in a violent skirmish at the top of the ridge you see to the southeast of us. But no one survived to tell us who killed her or why, and your Army denied knowing anything about it. I do know that it was after the war ended, so it makes even less sense. Who was she fighting? "We also know that my mother and her band of guerillas tracked and finally killed Colonel Maruyama and his Japanese troops deep in the jungle just as the war was ending. We also know that a bridge not far from the Japanese camp was dynamited a few days after the war ended killing several hundred Burmese civilians returning home from Yunnan; but no one has ever been able to identify who destroyed the bridge. It could not have been my mother's unit, because they had no explosives and no knowledge of how to use them if they had." I tried to look innocent, but it wasn't easy.

"I came over to meet you in hopes that you might be able to shed some light on the final chapter of my mother's life." He stared intently at me for several minutes.

Finally, ignoring the mayor's question, I asked, "So, was Duwa your father?"

"No, he was my stepfather. My mother told me that an English officer raped her when she was a teenager before the Japanese invaded, and I was the result. She consequently hated the English and anybody that looked like them. I was given to an aunt to raise, and I seldom saw my mother after the war started. She was too busy killing Japanese."

It finally made sense to me after all these years. "Okay." I tried to look innocent. "But why was her guerilla band made up entirely of women? Your book is very clear on that issue, I have never heard of women guerillas."

"Oh yes. They appear periodically throughout history. I believe the latest version became famous in Russia during the war. It's hard to explain, but I think the best way to describe it is through Rudyard Kipling and his poem, The Female of The Species is More Deadly Than The Male. I have forgotten much of it. But the last two verses are:

"My mother was very upset with our government and the compromise attitude we made with both the English and the Japanese invaders. She realized that the only way she could bring peace to Burma was to defeat our enemies by organizing the women of Burma. And she did. That is why she is a hero to all of us. What we men were not able to do, she and her compatriots came close to accomplishing at great sacrifice."

"I am sorry Mr. Mayor that I cannot offer anything that would help you complete your book. I only know what other soldiers told me about the legend of your mother." The mayor couldn't see that I had my fingers crossed behind my back.

FORTY-FOUR

It was early, but I downed another big breakfast to get started. I had borrowed a folding chair from the hotel and brought it with a bagged lunch to the American graveyard. I walked briskly to my friend's marker, opened the chair and sat down next to it. I took out my notebook and opened it up and glanced at my scribbles. "Boy, have I got a lot to tell you Phil. You won't believe what I found out yesterday." Nobody was around. I thought.

Before I could continue, I heard footsteps in the grass behind me. I turned around to see Mayor Maung walking briskly toward me with two burley Burmese men at his side. They slowed down and the two men stopped a few feet away. "Good morning Mr. Beltrans. It is good to see you again." I wasn't so sure I agreed. "May I join you?"

One of his bodyguards brought up a folding chair and the mayor sat down. "This is a beautiful place, isn't it? I love to sit here in the morning, before it gets hot." His smile was a little too agreeable for me.

"So you have been here before Mr. Mayor?" I was expressing friendliness that I didn't quite feel.

"Oh yes. I have come here often, particularly when I was writing my book. You see, I know everything about my mother except how she died and why, and I felt that the answer lay here, somewhere in this graveyard. But, of course, I never knew quite where to look until this morning. Thank you for leading me to the answer. Oh you don't have to deny anything Mr. Beltrans. I could tell by your body language yesterday that you knew more than you were admitting.

"So let's see what we have here." He rose from his chair and walked around looking down at the grave markers. "Umm. I notice something very interesting. Look here Ray, all of these men died on the same day in 1945, several weeks after the war ended. I wonder why that is. And here is a grave of someone who appears to be their commanding officer. He apparently died a day later. Was he wounded in the battle and then succumbed a day later of his wounds? But that can't be Ray. The war had ended a couple of weeks earlier. What are we looking at here Mr. Beltrans, some kind of a battle that was not recorded in the history books?"

I was never good at concealing a secret. I just stared down at the ground. The mayor walked back and sat down in his chair. He sat staring into space, as the sun got hotter. "I think I am beginning to see what happened.

"Burmese tending their rice paddies that day told of hearing gunfire coming from that ridge we see over there. It was a couple of weeks after the war ended. They say that a day later, they saw a worn-out group of what appeared to be ragtag American soldiers walking down from the mountain carrying their wounded and sick comrades. And a few days later, a group of American soldiers from Myitkyina marched up the hill with mules and came back carrying stretchers loaded with dead bodies.

"After that, your Army denied everything, even that it happened, although many civilians swear that they saw what I just described." Pointing to the markers, he said, "Here we are looking at the soldiers who were killed on that mountain, aren't we?" He folded his arms and glared at me.

"You know, Ray." He was getting more agitated as he talked. "That would answer the blown bridge too, wouldn't it? A group of Merrill's Marauders operating behind enemy lines that were just trying to get home after the war had ended. But why would they blow up a bridge and kill several hundred innocent civilians? And why would my mother want to kill them? Maybe the two things are related. We are asking more questions than we can answer, aren't we Ray? Maybe you could help me out here. I have got to find an ending to my book." He stared at me intently. I looked back over my shoulder to see his two bodyguards scowling at me.

FORTY-FIVE

I finally looked up, wiping away a tear. "If the American Army denies that a battle took place on that mountain, or that a group of Merrill's Marauders even existed in that jungle, we have one of two choices. Either the Army is right, and they did not exist, or there is a reason that they are trying to keep it a secret.

"Let's assume for the sake of argument that the second choice is true, and of course, I am not saying that it is. Then what happened on that hill and in that jungle is classified information. Divulging classified information is a federal offense punishable by many years in the federal pen.

"So you can see that even if I knew anything, I couldn't talk about it. Of course, there is always the possibility that the whole story is fiction and your mother died of malaria somewhere deep in the jungle." Now I was on a roll.

"However, I know that you want to know what actually happened to your mother and how to finish the last chapter of your book. So, let's make up a purely fictional story that is too fantastic to be true. I will start.

"Suppose this fictional American Army of yours that never existed had actually killed Colonel Maruyama and his men and had then started home when the war ended. Suppose also that your mother had joined up with them before that fatal battle and helped to wipe out the Japanese soldiers.

"Let's also suppose that the returning Americans had been told that the Burmese civilians who were trying to get home were actually Communist soldiers attempting to invade Burma by crossing that bridge. It would be obvious that the destruction of that bridge would save Burma from another invasion, hypothetically of course." The mayor was now writing frantically.

"And let's further suppose that the killing of the

I took almost an hour to relate my "fictional" story of an American Army group trying to work its way out of the Burmese jungle through hostile territory, fighting one battle after another and making decisions that resulted in the deaths of innocent civilians, including the mayor's mother. I emphasized the part where Nang was aiming her pistol at my head when she was killed. When I ended, I watched the mayor finish his writing.

"So how's that for a fictional story of a American Army that did not exist?" I smiled at him for the first time. The mayor glanced back over his notebook, sat it down and looked up at me. "It's an interesting story Ray, and too fantastic to be true, but I might use it to finish off my book." He closed his notebook. "I would like to send you a copy of it when I finish Mr. Beltrans. Could I do that?"

Before they got to the trees I yelled at him. "Mr. Mayor, if you want to visit your mother's burial spot, head along that trail you see in the southeast that leads up that mountain. When you reach the summit, you will see a rock outcropping about two hundred yards to your right. Walk over to the edge of the forest next to it and you will be very close to her last resting place. Hypothetically speaking of course." He stared back at me and I saw moisture in his eyes.

"I may just do that. I am much obliged to you Mr. Beltrans." He turned and continued on into the trees with his friends. I may have told him too much.

I stared after them for a few minutes. I then turned back to Phil's grave marker and pulled out my notebook. Opening it to the first page.

FORTY-SIX

Leaving Rangoon, I had taken a window seat on a 747, but I was not interested in looking out at the jungle as it passed by below. I was flying over Thailand, Vietnam and the Philippines on my way to Tokyo. I wanted to sleep; flights always go faster when you sleep. But there was too much going through my mind.

My son, Mark, had just been released from federal prison since his draft board had rejected his appeal that he would not bear arms to kill Vietnamese civilians. Mark had shown his support to his high school buddies who had listened to the Marine Corps sergeant who convinced them to join up. He met them at the train station as they came home and helped the wounded get off the train. His best friend had lost both of his legs in a landmine explosion in the Vietnamese jungle. Mark was working with him to help him learn to walk again. Mark had told me that he had never been kept awake at night by memories, as were many of his friends who had come home from the fighting in Southeast Asia.

It had been a stormy relationship between the two of us when Mark announced that he would not be drafted into the military for service in Vietnam. I could not understand my son's reluctance to serve our country. And yet, in a way, I could. Mark's argument was well reasoned and logical and I could see that my son was not trying to avoid serving his country. He was sincerely unwilling to kill people with whom he had no quarrel. I soon ran out of arguments except for the one that my son would serve time in the federal penitentiary if he refused to be inducted. Mark finally agreed that that was a possibility but said that he was willing to accept that fate if it was inevitable.

My wife and I visited our son in jail every few weeks, and now that he was out we had developed a sound and affectionate relationship. We had long discussions about moral and political subjects, and I was impressed with Mark's understanding and mature approach to world issues. I wondered why I hadn't noticed my son's depth and obvious intelligence before. I was happy when Mark was released and was particularly happy when Mark announced that he was going to college.

On my way to Burma, I had first flown to San Francisco where I stopped off to see Phil's wife Janice and meet her second husband. I had taken a cab to her home because she said she would not have recognized me at the airport.

"Hello Ray," said a middle aged, yet attractive, woman as she opened the front door. "You made it just when I expected you to. My God. I haven't seen you since, when was it, 1942? You and Phil sailed out of Fort Mason on a troop transport headed for India. That was the last time I saw both of you. No wait. You dropped the sword to us in 1945 on your way home. That was the last time I saw you.

I grimaced at the thought but smiled and offered her a firm handshake. "It seems like only yesterday," I added quickly. "My you look nice." I was not good at complimenting women on their looks.

"Thank you Ray," she said as a man walked up smiling. "I want you to meet my husband, Charlie." We exchanged pleasantries and sat down in the living room.

After a while, Janice sat up and looked me in the eye. "Ray, There is a reason that I asked you to stop by on your trip to Burma, other than the joy of seeing you again." She smiled and sat back to talk. "I want you to do me a favor on your trip to the Far East. Take a look at the mantle above the fireplace."

I looked up at the mantle as instructed. I gasped, rose off of the couch and walked over to it. I must have stared at the sword for a full minute, then with the deliberation of a warrior, reached up and lifted it off of its support blocks. I slowly pulled the blade out of its case, admiring the beautiful carvings and shape of this masterfully handcrafted weapon.

It had the typical curve created by the Japanese sword makers, caused by the differential cooling cycle the blade went through when it was heated and cooled during the manufacturing process. I had read somewhere that the curve of the blade was also the result of the different carbon content of the metal that had been forged together to make what was at the time, the most potent killing weapon in the world. I gently returned the sword to its place on the mantle. I slowly turned to Janice. "Why am I looking at Phil's sword on your mantle?"

"Well Ray, as you know, it is not Phil's sword. He took it from the Japanese colonel that you two executed, and you passed it on to me when you returned home in late 1945. I had this beautiful stand made, and it has sat here on my mantle ever since.

"My girls grew up with it, not daring to touch it, but never failing to admire it, almost daily. Guests that have visited us have all asked about it, its origin and how I became its owner. One of our guests was an expert on Japanese samurai swords and became entranced with it. He would take it out of its case and stare at it for hours. I think he would come over to visit us just so he could look at this sword.

"He recently told me that he thinks that it is a priceless relic of the early Yamato Period in ancient Japanese history. He thinks that someone in Japan owns it and wishes that he or she had it back. And that is where you come in Ray. Charlie and I and our two girls agree that this sword should be returned to its owner in Japan. We would like you to take it with you on your trip to Burma, stop in Japan and try to locate its owner."

I sat back down in the sofa and bit my lip, staring up at the sword. "This sword means a lot to me as you know Janice. Your husband, my best friend, gave his life for it. We endured hell that you will, fortunately, never experience. It is kind of a symbol of what we stood for in our fight to liberate the Burmese people from the Japanese, and I am very happy to know that it has been safely stored on your mantle all these years." The memories of my time in Burma with

Phil returned to me as I sat there looking at my friend's wife and her husband, not quite knowing what to say next.

"So let's start with that Ray. I am not going to live forever, and my girls, although it had been a part of their childhood, have no use for it. I can just see it being sold at an auction for pennies on the dollar to an unscrupulous dealer who knows its true value.

"But more importantly, what does this sword stand for? It stands for war, death and conflict. It was built during some war period in Japan's history, has probably killed dozens of its enemies and was strapped to the side of a Japanese officer who probably killed several hundred Burmese civilians. Every time I look at it, I see death. I want you to do me one last favor, Ray. Take it back to the descendents of its last owner and let them mount it above their fireplace. It will have far more significance to them." I sat back in the sofa again and stared at the sword. I had been caught completely off guard and had to agree with her. "Your are right, Janice. This sword has no meaning in our culture. It has meaning to me because I watched its owner die dangling at the end of a hangman's noose.

"Hanging is a terrible way to die. Colonel Maruyama would much rather have been allowed to take his own life with this beautiful weapon. But we wouldn't let him. He had shown no mercy to the people of Burma, and we would end his war for him the way we thought it should be ended."

We all sat there silently for a minute. "Death is never easy Janice, especially for those who watch it. This is particularly true when you are holding the hand of someone you love when he takes his last breath. I think, in the end, Phil was sorry that he had killed the colonel. He couldn't even watch the Japanese warrior gasp at the end as his neck broke. God, I wish we would stop going to war!"

FORTY-SEVEN

I was staring at the cloud cover below us as I felt the airliner slowly lose altitude on its decent into Narita Airport. Had I done the right thing to agree with Janice and return the colonel's sword to Japan? She had wrapped it in a fishing case that was originally designed to hold a fly rod. It was large enough to house the samurai sword without disclosing what it was. I could tell airport inspectors that I was visiting their country to do a little fly-fishing and maybe they would not ask me to open it. It had worked so far, but I was skeptical about Japan. Who ever went to Japan to fly fish? I thought. I'll be lucky to get by with that one.

What bothered me the most about my trip to Japan was that Janice had told the Japanese Counsel in San Francisco the approximate time when I would be arriving in Tokyo. She told them that I would be looking for the descendents of the colonel from whom Phil had taken the sword during the war. She couldn't remember the name of the colonel that her husband had executed, but I would know.

I wasn't sure why this was bothering me, but I wished that she had not alerted the Japanese government that I was on his way there with this priceless sword. She had told me that the person she had talked to in the office in San Francisco was apparently not too interested and suggested that I contact the proper authorities in Tokyo as they would help me find the colonel's descendents.

I stood at the arrival area in the airport watching the suitcases come into view. I couldn't help but look around me as I waited. I saw nothing that would alert me as my suitcase came out, and then I saw the fishing case come down the ramp. I walked over nonchalantly and picked them both up. I had added a sling to the rod case so that I could carry it over my shoulder.

After throwing the rod case on my shoulder, picking up my brief case and setting my suitcase on the floor, I grabbed its handle and looked at my fellow passengers retrieving their cases. Again I saw nothing suspicious as I looked around the concourse. I am being much too nervous, I thought. I walked toward the exit dragging my suitcase on its wheels and clutching my fly rod case slung over my shoulder. How am I going to find Colonel Maruyama descendents in a country that doesn't even speak English? I passed through customs without a problem and kept walking toward the door. I could see the taxis waiting outside along the curb.

As I reached the exit and walked into the sunshine, I became aware of two big Japanese men walking on either side of me. They were both well dressed in business suits carrying brief cases, obviously on their way to a meeting. But why were they walking so close to me?

As I stopped at the curb to hail a taxi, I felt strong hands under each elbow that pushed me along and kept me walking. I glanced at the first one and then the other, but they only looked straight ahead, now walking faster with me in tow. I had been trained to defend myself, but that was many years ago. These two guys seemed to be able to take care of themselves under any circumstances.

I thought it better to continue on as they pushed me away from the concourse and toward the parking lot. A car drove up, a back door opened, and I was pushed into it. One of my escorts moved in beside me, and the door closed. The car sped off as I noticed that they were driving on the wrong side of the road. That was the last I saw of anything for awhile that morning as my bodyguard tied a bandana around my eyes and put handcuffs on my wrists,

"Welcome Captain Beltrans. We have been awaiting your arrival for some time now, but we Japanese are very patient," a short middle-aged Japanese man was sitting behind a desk as I was escorted into his office. I hadn't been called "captain" for many years, and the word startled me. I was pushed into a chair that was across from the speaker. Someone removed my handcuffs and blindfold. I blinked and tried to focus on the man in front of me.

"You may call me Mr. Izuma and I will call you Ray, if that is okay with you." I did not like his smile. "I must say, it was very kind of you to alert us that you were coming to Japan with your treasure," he pointed to the rod case that I was now gripping tightly. "It has saved us a great deal of work."

"We are not interested in you," Mr. Izuma responded. "We are interested in that samurai sword you are carrying. First of all, we know that it doesn't belong to you, nor to Mrs. Jenkins, or whatever her new name is. It belongs to a Japanese Army officer from whom you took it during the war."

That's interesting, I thought. He doesn't know Colonel Maruyama's name, or he would have used it.

"You see, we all belong to a Japanese organization, whose name does not concern you, that is dedicated to retrieving all of the samurai swords lost to Allied forces during the war. If you recall, your General MacArthur ordered all of the soldiers under his command to return or not accept swords from Japanese officers that had been offered as a token of our surrender when the war ended. Most of your officers complied with the general's orders, but some did not.

"Strangely enough, most who kept the surrendered swords were in the China-Burma Theater of operations, and most of those were British officers. Starting at the top, Lord Mountbatten ignored MacArthur's order and set the stage for other officers in his command to do the same. A few American officers also kept their swords, including you, Captain Beltrans." His eyes had a much more intense glare about them.

Before I could respond, Mr. Izuma continued, "Ah yes, I know. Your unit was somewhere in the Burmese jungle when it all ended, and you didn't get the word. Or was it that you hated the Japanese so badly that you intentionally ignored your general's order? It doesn't matter, captain. You and your sword are here now, and it is time to take a look at it." I instinctively pulled the case back out of Mr. Izuma's reach.

"Come, come, Ray. You can neither hide it nor use it as a defense weapon. Just pass it across the desk, please." He patience was obviously wearing thin.

"Yes, you are right, Mr. Izuma. This sword does not belong to me. But my life does. I would like to know what you intend to do with me if I give you this sword."

"Unfortunately Ray, your life is not a bargaining chip and is entirely in my hands. If the sword is of minor value, one that was made in the, say, Meiji Period, the nineteenth century, I will return it to you and you can be on your way. If it was made during the early Edo period, or maybe earlier, your life will be forfeited, because, of course, we can't have you running around telling the authorities who stole the sword. But we won't know until we see it, will we? So hand it over Ray and let's take a look at it."

I reluctantly set it on the desk and Mr. Izuma slowly opened the rod case. It was well wrapped to protect a priceless treasure or a fishing rod. I smiled as Mr. Izuma reached the end. He finally opened the inner case, reached in and pulled out----a fishing rod. Everyone in the room gasped, and Mr. Izuma fell back into his chair looking at me.

I smiled. "Isn't that the best looking fly rod you have ever seen?"

FORTY-EIGHT

Mr. Izuma continued to pace back and forth across the room. "Okay, Ray. Let's solve this problem. I want the sword and you want your life. It seems to me that we could reach an agreement that would satisfy both of our wants."

I couldn't restrain a smile. "You missed that one Mr. Izuma. Let's restate the facts. Yes, I want my life, but your desire to get your hands on the sword has no relevance to the issue before us. I am the only one alive who knows where the sword is or how to get control of it. If anything happens to me, you will never see it again. That sort of reduces our options, doesn't it?

"The only chance you have to get your hands on it is to let me go and hope that I will lead you to it. It seems to me that you have no other choice. Don't you agree?"

The room was quiet for several more minutes as Mr. Izuma returned to his chair, sat down and stared at me. "Yes, you o seem to have the winning hand, but the game isn't over. I will have scouts looking for you all over Japan, and at some point, you will have to retrieve that sword. When you do, your life will be over. That sounds like a fair exchange now doesn't it Ray?"

I nodded without saying anything. Mr. Izuma looked at his two accomplices; they stood up and put the blindfold back over my eyes, helped me stand up and walked me out of the building and into a car. Before we left the room, I turned back and said, "Oh, by the way, you can keep the fly rod." All I heard was some incoherent swearwords in Japanese.

When we arrived at my hotel, Mr. Izuma's man took my blindfold off and opened the car door. I walked out into the warm air and into the lobby. Ideas were spinning through my mind as I walked, but nothing seemed to be appropriate. I had to think as I walked up to the lobby desk. As I took my room key, smiling at the girl behind the counter, she handed me an envelope.

I tore open the envelope and read the note. "Please stop by our office. I want to talk with you; you don't need to call, just come by." Someone in the American Ambassador's office signed it.

Fortunately, the taxi driver knew the address and it didn't take long to get there. I paid him and walked up the steps, through the main door and into the big office. The receptionist ushered me into a small meeting room and asked me to wait a minute, closing the door behind her. I sat patiently wondering what this was all about.

After a few minutes, the door opened and a well dressed American walked in, followed by several assistants, including a Japanese man. After introductions, they all sat down around the meeting table.

"Mr. Beltrans, thank you for coming. We have a problem that we wanted to talk over with you. Did you have a nice trip from Burma? Good!" he said as I nodded reluctantly.

"The problem revolves around the sword you brought with you. It is safely stored in your hotel I assume."

I smiled and nodded.

"Good. It seems that it is more important than you probably know. Let me explain.

"Are you familiar with the Japanese ultra nationalist movement that has sprung up here since the end of World War II? Actually it has been in existence for several hundred years, but it has become more active in the last few years. Here they are known as Uyoku Dantai groups, and their aim is to return Japan to their pre-war goal of military dominance. The group with which we are most concerned is called Yukoku Doshikal. We understand that they intend to hold a big unveiling ceremony at the Yasukuni Shrine when they get your sword. As you know, the Yasukuni Shrine is dedicated to the brave Japanese soldiers who gave their lives for the Emperor during the World War II.

"The sword will be their relic, it is their shin-uyoku symbolizing their break with the United States. This ancient sword is their link to the past, and symbolizes their desire to return to kokutai-goji, the fundamental character of Japan that they feel has been abandoned since the war.

"So you ask, what does this all have to do with your samurai sword? The sword is important to them because it represents all they stand for: war, aggression and military dominance. They would love to get their hands on it to symbolically emphasize their goals. But why do they want your sword?

"The Japanese government has kept track of the samurai swords lost during the war and has identified almost all of them. Some have been returned to their Japanese owners, and their new American owners have retained some. However, some are unaccounted for, and a few of these are very expensive.

"You may have heard about the Japanese friend of Mrs. Jenkins who visited her home in San Francisco. He noted that the sword was of impressive quality and notified the Japanese government that it may be one that was made during the late sixteenth or early seventeenth centuries. That would coincide with several swords that we know are still missing or unaccounted for. So we need to look at it and make identification before it falls into ultra nationalistic hands. We are happy that we got to you before the Yukoku Doshikal did."

I smiled and added, "So am I."

"Consequently, we need you to give us the sword before it falls into their hands," the ambassador said. "I notice that you don't have it with you. Can you get it for us?"

I stared down at the table for a while, and then looked up at the ambassador. "My friend and I killed the owner of this sword in time of war after months of searching and fighting in several bloody battles. Now that war is over, both Phil's wife and I think it should be returned to its original owner. I am certain that if Phil were here he would agree. Consequently, I intend to locate its owner and give it to him or her. What happens to it after that is beyond my control."

"Mr. Beltrans, I understand your feelings, but there is much more at stake here. Japan is now our friend and we are obligated to help our ally in any way we can. This ultra nationalistic movement is what caused them to start World War II, and we can't let it get a foothold again. This sword of yours may be the link that they need to the past militaristic attitudes that would plunge us all into World War III. We can't take a chance on that."

"I understand your concerns Mr. Ambassador, but my mind is made up. However I will do all I can to keep the sword from falling into the wrong hands." I rose and walked out the door and onto the street. I hailed a taxi and headed back to my hotel once again.

FORTY-NINE

I sat at the hotel bar enjoying a scotch as I glanced over at the people sitting at the tables. Some were talking and some were reading newspapers. I was sure that they were all watching me, but was I being too suspicious? I finished my drink, stood up and walked slowly to the door. I looked into the glass on the door to see if it reflected anyone walking behind me. Nothing looked out of the ordinary.

I asked the taxi driver to take me to the Ginza District where I thought I could jump into another taxi and evade anyone who was following me. After all, every foreign tourist goes to the Ginza when visiting Tokyo.

I jumped out of the cab and walked briskly along the sidewalk through a huge throng of people moving in all directions. I had no idea where I was. I finally saw an empty taxi and hailed it.

I gave the driver an address that was several blocks from my destination. I slipped down in the back seat so that I would not be recognized by anyone on the street.

When we arrived at the address, I jumped out and paid the driver. I stood on the sidewalk for a moment to see if anyone had been following us. I finally turned and walked down the block to a dim side street. Turning into it, I walked for several more blocks stopping periodically to look behind me. I was in a residential or light industrial area and there was almost no one on the street. I pulled out my scrap of paper and studied the address. It wasn't far now.

I knocked faintly at the old wooden door, one that looked like it had been built over a hundred years ago. I searched up and down the street as I waited for someone to answer my knock. I was about ready to knock again when the door slowly opened. "Hello. I am looking for Mr. Akihira, Mr. Miyairi Akihira." The door opened slowly, and an elderly lady dressed in a traditional Japanese robe motioned me to enter. It was impossible to see in the dark room. I stood waiting for my eyes to adjust and soon sensed that the woman had turned and walked out the back door. I looked around as my eyes began to focus in the darkness.

Soon a young man walked into the room. He had on a machinist's apron and rather dirty clothes. He was obviously a journeyman. "Good morning sir. May I help you?"

"Yes. I am looking for Mr. Akihairi. My name is Ray Beltrans from the United States. Mr. Akihairi will know who I am."

"Ah yes, Mr. Beltrans. My Name is Suzuki, and I have been expecting you. Unfortunately, Mr. Akihairi died a few weeks ago, and I have replaced him as the master sword maker in the shop." He bowed low. "Please sit down."

I was shocked but did as I was told. "I have been looking forward to visiting with Mr. Akikairi. Did you receive the package I sent him?" Mr. Suzuki smiled and turned to walk out the back door. I could see better now and concluded that I was in the middle of a machine shop or a small blacksmith shop. I could see the furnace over in the corner and an anvil close by. There was a small fire in the furnace keeping the room warmer than it needed to be. Mr. Suzuki returned with a package under his arm.

I took the package and opened it revealing its content, a beautifully constructed samurai sword inside a classic sheath. I pulled the sword out, but only about a quarter of the way. I smiled and put the sword away. "Yes, this is the sword I sent you. Did you read the letter I enclosed with it?"

"Yes, Mr. Beltrans, I did. However, I was interested to know why you sent the sword to Mr. Akikairi or to me. He may be the most famous maker of samurai swords in Japan, but we don't deal in used swords. Your letter did mention that you intended to return it to its rightful owner, so I assume that you want us to date it and then help you locate its owner. Is that correct?"

"Yes, Mr., Suzuki, that's basically what I had in mind."

"I have been very busy in making swords for customers here in Japan, so I have not had time to look closely at it. I doubt if I can be of much help to you, but let me take a look." Mr. Suzuki reached out, took the package and carefully removed the sword. He turned it over in his hands and scanned the blade, hilt and handle slowly. He turned to his desk and pulled out a magnifying glass and used it to look more closely at what was obviously a beautiful relic. Several minutes passed making me a little nervous.

"I must express my embarrassment to you Mr. Beltrans. I had assumed when I read your letter that this was probably a recently constructed or perhaps cheap imitation of the ancient weapons that have been in existence here for hundreds of years. We have many of these here in Japan. Consequently, I did not bother to look at it closely. Now that I have, I can see that it is much more than an imitation.

"It was probably built in the late sixteenth or early seventeenth century, the Ido Period, by one of the great sword makers in Japan You can see by the engraving on the hilt that the steel used in its construction originated in the famous Tatara Iron Works. No other steel in Japan could match its quality for use in building the samurai sword.

"Swords made from Tatara steel are the best because they could control the carbon content of their product very closely. The carbon content is critical in the sword's manufacture, and even the best sword maker will fail if the ingredients in the steel are not perfect. The steel is heat-treated and cooled at just the right rate; the material is then forged by hand, folded back on itself and then heated again. It is a laborious process that takes many years to learn and perfect. I have been in training for over twenty years with Mr. Akihira, acknowledged to be the greatest modern day Japanese sword maker. I am now just making the first swords on my own after the death of my great master." He bowed his head for a few seconds.

Mr. Suzuki finally wrapped the sword in its cloth and replaced it into its casing. Before doing so, he ran his figure lightly across its sharp blade. A spot of blood appeared on his hand. "Do you know the ancient belief that it is bad luck to remove a samurai sword from its scabbard without drawing blood?"

"No, I haven't heard that superstition before." I couldn't help but wonder how much bad luck I had built up over the years with Phil's sword!

"As I look at this sword, I have answered my second question, which is why did you send it directly to me and not just carry it with you. This sword has enormous value, both monetarily and symbolically to our country. I won't even guess how much money it could bring on the black market.

"Your letter mentioned that the owner of the sword in San Francisco had alerted the Japanese government that you were bringing it with you on your trip back from Burma. I recognize now that you must have feared that her message may have alerted people in Japan who would like very much to get their hands on it. You trusted that I would not immediately recognize its value, or that I was too honest to take full advantage if it."

"So, what do you intend to do with it now that you know its value, Mr. Beltrans?"

I stared down at the sword lying across his lap in its shipping box. My mind wondered back to Burma, the dozens of graves in the memorial park in Myitkyina, the intensity of the Burmese women fighting for their homeland and to Nang's son, trying to make sense of it all in his book.

One who has not killed with it would not understand the significance of this beautifully built weapon. Who would understand the joy and then the horror of having just killed someone in self-defense? But after all, isn't that what all killing is, self defense. Some unknown man, perhaps five hundred years ago, devoted a better part of his life forming this sword out of hot steel, pounding and shaping it and putting his heart and soul into a weapon whose only use was to kill. It was designed only to support Bushito, the way of the warrior. What do we Americans know of Bushido? I asked myself.

I first met Bushido in Burma when my unit was attacked by a group of suicidal Japanese soldiers charging into our murderous gunfire at the battle of Myitkyina. A young officer waiving his samurai sword, screaming and running at me with no possibility of success or survival led them.

As the Japanese troops lay dead and dying in front of me, I had walked up to look down at the young officer bleeding to death on the ground. The sight of this young man dying in front of me with his sword in his hand was etched in my memory. I remembered the expression in his eyes as death approached, perhaps wondering if dying for the emperor was really worth it.

So this is what Bushito is, I thought as I watched the soldier gasp his last breath. I remember looking around at the other Japanese who had sacrificed their lives that day and wondered what their families thought. We will never know. I shook my head and returned to my cover to await the next attack.

"I intend to locate the family who owns this sword, and return it to them and apologize for killing their ancestor on the field of battle." After thinking for a minute, I added, "But I think I will embellish his death a little when I find his descendents. There is no need for them to know the exact truth," as I envisioned the colonel dangling from a hangman's noose.

"You gave me the name of its owner in your letter, a Colonel Maruyama, I believe. I took the liberty of searching for his name here in Japan." Mr. Suzuki turned to sit down. "Unfortunately, there were two Colonel Maruyamas in the war, and one general by that name. The general was famous for being unable to retake Henderson Field on Guadalcanal in 1942; one of the colonels was in Manchuria and yours in Burma. I have been able to isolate your colonel's descendents as living in Kyoto but do not know their address. I suggest that you and I travel there and see what we can find.

"You do know that there are several organizations here in Japan that would kill to get this sword. For this reason, I assume that you are being followed; we need to travel to Kyoto separately. As a sword maker, the fact that I am carrying a sword with me should raise no suspicions. I suggest that you take the bullet train this evening, I'll take it this afternoon, and we'll meet in the bar at the Miyako Hotel. Remember, there are two Miyako Hotels in Kyoto. We will meet at the one in downtown, not the one at the train station."

"Sounds good to me." I shook his hand and walked out into the sunlight. I looked up and down the street but saw no one. I headed toward the main street to find a cab.

FIFTY

"What do you mean you lost him? You have never lost anyone in your lives. You damn idiots!"

"He disappeared in the crowds at the Ginza, and he must have taken a cab from there. We were not able to find him after that, Sir"

After calming down a minute, Mr. Izuma spoke up, "Okay, let's put our heads together and figure out where he would have sent that sword. He did not send it to his hotel or to the embassy, and he doesn't know anyone here in Tokyo. So where would he have sent it? Where would a sword not be conspicuous or cause a stir when it arrived and would still be there when he arrived to pick it up?

"Of course! We certainly overlooked the obvious didn't we? The only place in Tokyo that fits all those requirements is the shop of the most famous sword maker in Japan, Miyairi Akihira."

"But Mr. Izuma. Mr. Akihira died several weeks ago. Don't you remember reading that in the paper?"

"Yes, you fool that's true, but Beltrans would not have known that, and the great sword master would have had an apprentice, a man who has probably taken over his business. Let's find our where his shop is and pay the new owner a little visit."

Mrs. Suzuki heard a load banging at the door, and walked slowly toward the entrance. She opened the door carefully as was her custom, but someone on the outside shoved it hard and pushed her back. She was startled to see three men rudely push past her and into the shop.

She raised herself up to her full five foot one and asked what they wanted. The men looked around the shop letting their eyes accustom to the darkness. "Who is the master of this shop now that Mr. Akihira has died?" She couldn't tell who was speaking.

"My son, Akihiro Suzuki, is the new master of this shop."

"Where is he?"

"He left the shop early this afternoon." "And where did he go?"

"I don't know. He took his suitcase with him." "Did he take any swords with him?"

She paused for a moment. "Yes. He took several swords with him, but he did not tell me where he was going. He said he would be back in a few days." She felt a hand grab her throat.

FIFTY-ONE

"The Miyako is one of the best hotels I have ever seen," I said looking out the window at the Kyoto skyline and the mountain range in the background.

"Yes, which is why I suggested that we stay here. I have made and sold more swords to residents of this city than to people living anywhere else in Japan. But that is to be expected because of the great Zen Buddhist tradition here. If we have time, we must visit one of the ancient temples in the city.

"One of the great restraints that your country showed during the war was to put Kyoto off limits to your bombers. Consequently, the temples survived and are here today to be admired by our descendants and your tourists."

"But what do Buddhist temples have to do with our samurai sword," I asked looking down at Mr. Suzuki's sword carrying case sitting on his bed?

"The life of the samurai warrior was based on Zen Buddhism. The connection is probably not obvious to you Americans, but it is total and complete. Before we leave this beautiful city, I hope we have time to visit one of the Zen gardens here. To you, the sword is a symbol of war and violence. To us, it is not only a symbol of our past and culture; it is a symbol of peace and tranquility, as is Zen.

"I know that doesn't square with your experiences in World War II, but it is true. This is also true of the martial arts. Even though the use of the samurai sword and the martial arts seem violent to you, they are the ultimate manifestation of inner peace and harmony. I wish you could witness a display of the sword other than being attacked in a banzai charge. I am sure that your colonel was skilled in its use. It is probably very fortunate for you that you did not allow him to demonstrate, however.

"Consequently, I am very happy that you wish to return this sword to its rightful owner. If we can ever find the family, I want to see the expression on their faces when you present it to them after all these years."

I smiled, "Yes. So do I."

"Okay, let's begin our search in the phone book. I will do the calling. Let me see," mumbled Mr. Suzuki as he began thumbing through the Kyoto phone book. He picked up the phone, dialed and began talking in Japanese. I turned my chair toward the window where I could admire the town's beauty while I waited. There were lots of Maruyamas in the phone book, so the calling took a while. Each time, Mr. Suzuki hung up with a disappointed look on his face, and each time he picked up the phone and tried again.

After an hour or so of phoning, he had reached the last Maruyamas and turned to me. "Well, no one would admit that they were related to our deceased colonel." We stared out the window for a while. "Wait a minute Ray. The third call was a voice of an older woman, and she paused for maybe five or six seconds before answering, like she had to think about it. Everyone else answered immediately. I think it may be worth following up with her."

"Okay, let's do it!" Mr. Suzuki wrote down the address and we both jumped up and headed out the door.

The cab stopped and let us out along an old street lined with trees and homes built many years ago. I could not tell how old they were, but they were obviously built before the war. I thought of Mr. Suzuki's remarks that the 1.S. Air Corps was not allowed to bomb this city. What a good idea that was.

I rapped softly on the door. It was soon opened by a middle-aged man who bowed to the two men at his door. "Good morning sir," speaking in Japanese. "My name is Suzuki and my American friend here is Mr. Beltrans. Do you speak English?"

"Yes I do, a little broken maybe, but I think tolerable. Please come in. We have been expecting you. My name is Hiroki Maruyama; this is my wife Aiko and my daughter Chika. Please sit down."

The two men walked in with Suzuki carrying the sword case. They glanced at each other in amazement. I spoke first. "You say you were expecting us?"

"Yes, of course, but first, can I get you a cup of tea?" "No, thank you. Please tell us why you were expecting us. We just arrived here in Kyoto yesterday and didn't know that we were coming here until an hour ago," Mr. Suzuki replied.

Mr. Maruyama smiled. "Yes, that is true. But my mother, who answered the phone when you called this morning, sensed that you did not believe her and would be here soon. She immediately called me at work and asked me to come by to greet you when you arrived. We do not know, of course, what you want with us, but it apparently has something to do with my father, Colonel Maruyama. Did you know him?" he asked looking at me.

I thought quickly, opened my mouth, but soon closed it. I couldn't decide whether to lie or not. Before I could answer, the side door to the living room slid open and an elderly Japanese lady with snow-white hair slipped into the room. She bowed to us and turned to her son. "This is my mother gentleman, Kasuko Maruyama. She is the wife of the late Colonel." Everyone bowed to each other. "She understands English, but does not speak it. I will translate for her."

"She has been listening to our conversation and wants me to encourage you, Mr. Beltrans, to speak the truth. She sensed that you were contemplating telling us a false story in answer to my question. We have never heard how or where my father died and would very much appreciate knowing the truth. We can handle it." Madam Maruyama sat down on a mat and stared at me.

I looked around at everyone sitting in the room, particularly the colonel's pretty young granddaughter. How sad he couldn't have been here when she was born and couldn't watch her grow up. How terrible war is; I thought again of General Sherman's pronouncement as I stared at her.

"Colonel Maruyama was a brave and skillful soldier. He led his men at the battle of Myitkyina, Burma, and we fought against him for several months throughout the summer of 1944. When it finally became obvious that the Allied forces would prevail, your husband rallied a group of three hundred remaining soldiers and led them southeast into the Burmese jungle. They were battered and defeated, but he organized them and gave them hope as they regrouped into a formidable force.

"My unit was formed and trained specifically to find and kill him. I was the executive officer of a one hundred–fifty-soldier Special Forces group that tracked the colonel and his men for almost a year. We finally caught him and wiped out his entire unit just before the was ended." I paused and looked around the room to see if anyone believed me.

The colonel's son turned back away from his mother and said to me, "My mother says that you are leaving a whole lot out. She again asks you to share all the details with us. How did he die?"

"He was shot and killed leading a banzai charge against us with the last of his soldiers." I thought a minute. "My commander, Major Jenkins, was also killed in that attack, and I took over command of the unit."

"My mother wants to know how one hundred-fifty Americans were able to kill three hundred Japanese in the Burmese jungle."

"We set up a trap and killed a majority of them in a classic ambush." I then added quickly, "We had a big advantage over the Japanese forces. They did not know that we were in the area so they did not take proper precautions. We struck suddenly with a surprise attack from which your troops could not recover. It was rather like the battle of Midway when our naval forces were able to sink your carriers before Admiral Nagumo knew we were within a thousand miles of him." I hoped I looked sincere enough for the colonel's wife to believe me.

It was quiet in the room for a while. I hoped that I would not have to go into any more detail. I studied her face for signs that she believed me, but she showed no expression that I could detect. I thought how many times I had lied about the war. Truth is the first victim of war. I have forgotten who first said that.

"Mother wants to know where he is buried," Mr. Maruyama asked.

"All I can say is, somewhere in the Burmese jungle. There was no way we could have carried three hundred bodies for five hundred miles, so we buried them all on the spot where they were killed." Madam Maruyama nodded slowly.

"So why are you here today, Mr. Beltrans? You did not travel all this way just to tell us how my father died."

"You are right Mr. Maruyama.' I looked over at Mr. Suzuki as the master sword maker began to open his carrying case. "I came into possession of your father's sword after my commander was killed and gave it to his wife when I returned to the states. Now she and I would like to return it to you, its rightful owners. Mrs. Jenkins has kept it since the war, mounted on her mantel, but has now asked me to return it to you. I asked Mr. Suzuki here to help me find you, and here we are."

Mr. Suzuki pulled the sword, still in its scabbard, out and held it up for all to see. There was a loud gasp in the room. Everyone stood up and moved in closer to see and touch their family relic that had been missing since the war. Everyone said something in Japanese that made Mr. Suzuki smile. Madam Maruyama stood and reached in and gently took it in her hands. She pulled it close to her chest as tears rolled down her cheeks. Her son and granddaughter hugged her gently.

FIFTY-TWO

They didn't bother knocking and just pushed the door open with a bang. Everyone turned to the front door in time to see three men enter, dressed in business suits. Mr. Izuma was in the lead.

"So we meet again Mr. Beltrans. And I assume that this is Mr. Suzuki, and of course, the Maruyama family. Please accept my appreciation for leading us to the sword that I so badly want to possess. Please sit down." They all moved to the nearest chair. Madam Maruyama tightly clutched the sword as she sat back on her mat.

"The funny part of this whole caper is that none of you knows the significance of this sword sitting on her lap. Maybe Mr. Suzuki does."

Mr. Suzuki squirmed in his chair and looked back at the sword. "Oh, I think by the look on his face that he has been hiding something from the rest of you, haven't you?" Mr. Suzuki didn't answer.

"I, however, am not reluctant to 'spill the beans', as you Americans say. This sword, now sitting on the madam's lap, is the most famous and expensive relic in Japan. It is a national treasure, known as the Honjo Masamune sword, made by the absolute master sword maker in all of Japanese history, Goro Myuda Masamune. No one knows the exact date of its manufacture, but it was obviously built during the Kamakura era, probably around 1300. Master Masamune developed a double quenching process in making his swords that no one since has been able to duplicate.

"Mr. Suzuki can testify that the key to a fine samurai sword is the relative hardness and toughness of the steel. The blade itself must be able to be honed and keep a sharp edge, and the upper side of the sword must be tough enough to resist the battering a sword must withstand during battle. "Unfortunately for sword makers, these two characteristics are the exact opposite of each other in terms of carbon content of the steel and in quenching process. Master Masamune never disclosed his quenching technique, and sword makers for the last seven hundred years have been trying to duplicate his process to no avail. So all we have left of his sword building skill is the master sword of the Japanese people, the one sitting on madam's lap.

"The sword disappeared at the end of the war, and no one has been able to locate it since. We traced it to Burma, but beyond that, we could only guess that some American officer had taken it back home with him. Our contacts in San Francisco alerted us that it might be the one returning to Japan with Mr. Beltrans. Fortunately, our contacts were right.

"To answer your question, there is no way anyone can put a price on this sword. Suffice to say that I have been offered enough gold to make its capture worth my efforts. No, I am not some ultra nationalist radical. Politics is much too boring for me. With the money we will be paid for this sword, the three of us can retire and live our lives in comfort. Unfortunately for all of you, I cannot allow anyone else in this room to survive. Please rise and follow us out to our car. It is just large enough to hold all of us in comfort." Mr. Izuma smiled at his small joke.

He turned to grab my arm and that of Mr. Suzuki to march us out the door. And then it happened in a time frame of probably two seconds or less. The first thing I saw was a blinding flash of steel headed toward Mr. Izuma. With incredible speed, it severed his head, bouncing it along the floor. With equal dexterity, the sword pulled back and, with a swift backhand swipe, sliced though the stomach of the first bodyguard, spilling his intestines on the floor and causing him to scream in pain as he collapsed.

With the sword now cocked behind her, Madam Maruyama lunged straight at the second bodyguard, shoving the blade straight trough his stomach and out his back. She just as quickly pulled the blade out of his body and stepped back so that he could drop to the floor unimpeded. There was no sound except for the gushing of blood onto the floor. Everyone looked at Madam Maruyama as she wiped the blood from the blade with her handkerchief.

I looked at her wondering if she were going to take revenge on her husband's killer next. But she smiled at me and said in halting English, "At least there will be no bad luck in this house today." She put the sword back into its scabbard and clutched it to her body, closing her eyes and looking up to heaven with tears rolling down her cheeks.

She finally looked at her family and said, "You probably didn't know that women can be samurai too. My husband trained me well. I miss him so much."

She then turned and pointed to the far wall, to the mantle over the small fireplace. I squinted to see what I had not noticed since I had been there. It was a beautiful sword holder sitting on the mantle, shaped perfectly to hold a curved samurai sword. But it was empty.

Madam Maruyama said nothing but slowly extended the sword in its scabbard to me and pointed again to the mantle. "It has been empty since my husband left for the war. Would you please set his sword back on its holder where it belongs?"

Startled, I walked over to the fireplace and, with great care lifted the sword onto its holder. I found myself bowing to the most beautiful killing machine ever made. I had never bowed this low before but couldn't resist. I wondered if Colonel Maruyama was looking down at me. I turned, reached out and lifted Chika so that she could touch her grandfather's sword. "This has been in your family for seven hundred years," I whispered in her ear and stroked her hair to calm her from the trauma she had just witnessed. I didn't know if she understood me, but she smiled.

There was a loud noise at the now open front door as everyone looked up to see what was happening. In walked the American ambassador and three policemen followed by several Japanese dignitaries. "Okay, what do we have here?"

FIFTY-THREE

I asked, "Do you think Madam Maruyama believed my story about her husband's killing?"

"No, I don't think so Ray," Mr. Suzuki responded with a smile. "I am sure, however, that she appreciated your attempt to make him appear more heroic than he probably was. We all have read the history of the Japanese occupation of Burma during the war and how brutal our troops were to the civilians there.

"I am sure she detected that you did not say why the American forces would have gone to the trouble of organizing and training a unit of Merrill's Marauders just to kill Colonel Maruyama; after all, he was just holed up in the jungle waiting for the war to end. Someday I would like to hear the real story from you Ray."

I nodded and added, "By the way, how is your mother doing?"

"She is just fine, thank you. I called my wife yesterday and alerted her to mom's condition so she could take her to the hospital. She had minor wounds on her neck and face but is recovering fine. I will drop in and see her tomorrow when I return to Tokyo."

"Now tell me about this beautiful place in which we are walking," I asked.

"This is the Daisen-In Garden in the Daitoku-ji Temple. This temple is the headquarters of the Rinzai Sect of Zen Buddhism here in Japan and is one of the most beautiful rock gardens you will find anywhere in the world.

"I brought you here because this temple was first built in 1319, close to the year in which our famous sword was constructed. I want you to experience the similarities between the garden and the sword. Unfortunately, the temple was burned down in a war in the fifteenth century, but was rebuilt in 1477. Most of the buildings you see here are from that period. Let's sit down over here and experience the beauty and tranquility of this garden.

"Yes, I admit that I didn't tell you the whole truth about the sword in Tokyo. I was afraid that if you knew its real value, you would take it back home and sell it on the black market. I totally under estimated your honesty and determination to have it returned to its rightful owner. For this gross misjudgment I sincerely apologize." He bowed low to me and I smiled in appreciation.

We sat quietly for a while staring at the simple, yet elegant, design of the most beautiful garden I had ever seen. "How did your family survive the bombing during the war? I assume that you lived in Tokyo at the time."

"My mother and I obviously survived, but my father, brothers and sisters did not. They were burned to death during the infamous firebombing raid in the spring of 1945. We don't know the exact number, but there were well over a hundred thousand civilians killed that night.

"When the first bombs landed, my mother scooped me up and ran for the river that runs through that the city which was used as a water source for fire protection. She held me tight and jumped into the river keeping us both covered with water as the flames swept around us.

"We almost didn't survive because the fire soaked up most of the oxygen in the air. Fortunately, a light breeze came up and blew the fire back over the buildings it had already burned, and we survived. Unfortunately, the rest of my family did not. We never found their bodies."

I was stunned into silence. I stared at the centuries old rock garden in front of me trying to put the pieces of this man's life and culture together.

"No doubt you are wondering why I helped you and didn't kill you when I had the chance," he said with a smile. "The answer lies in front of you Ray.

"Let's back up a minute," Mr. Suzuki continued. "Yesterday, you looked at the face of a samurai warrior who, after she dispatched the three gangsters, as you Americans would call them, could have killed you as easily as stepping on a bug. Did you see the expression on her face when she looked in your eyes? Remember what she has been through.

"She was widowed as a teenage bride with a small child to raise and without a loving husband to help her. I'll bet she's spent every night since then praying for the time when his killer would come to her door and beg her for forgiveness. She could almost feel the sensation of running that sword through your stomach and watching in pleasure as your life left your body; she would have looked up to heaven and said, your death has been avenged.

"I'll bet you anything that she came here to this shrine at least once a week since the war, praying for the opportunity that would free her soul and let her descendents live in peace. But when she sat, probably exactly where you are sitting now, she looked at the tranquility that humans can create and found that peace does not come with revenge. We discover it when we accept the love and tranquility existing in the soul of humanity that this garden represents. She won, not because she killed you, but because she could have, but did not.

"You gave her the greatest gift of all. You gave her the chance to avenge her husband's death, but she did not take it. Her inner peace and wisdom prevailed, and she doused the flames of anger that had raged in her since 1945.

"I suspect, Ray, that she was haunted by the old Zen saying, 'You are not punished for your sins, you are punished by them.' She was not going to live the rest of her life knowing that she had killed someone for the sake of revenge. What could be a greater sin?

"I do not have that luxury. I will never have the chance to confront the pilot that dropped those firebombs on my family. He may not have even survived the war. But, if he is alive, does he lie awake at night crying over killing my family? Maybe he does, but I doubt it."

Pointing to the beautiful landscape surrounding us, he said, "Do you Americans have an equivalent 'garden of peace' to which you can escape? I understand that there are some beautiful, even breathtaking sights in the states of California, Utah, Arizona and New Mexico created by nature. Where would you go, Ray, to experience a peaceful wonder like this, where you could search and meditate, to eventually become secure with your inner wisdom and learn your true inner nature, as Madam Maruyama has done? I hope you can find such a place when you return home.

"How many lives must we live before we realize that each of us is responsible for the sins we commit, for the evil we permit to happen. The 'I was only following orders' excuse, whether the orders were from God or a commanding officer, will not do when you have to answer the ultimate question. When the call came, how did you respond?

"I suspect that madam Maruyama has fought with her inner demons ever since the war. If you had come here even five years ago, I believe that you would now be lying headless on her living room floor. Who can predict when each of us will attain true wisdom, or if ever, in this life?"

After a while, I finally asked, "Okay, but how does that sword fit into all of this?"

"When a samurai holds a sword like that one in her hands, she has the ultimate control over life and death in the world around her. She does not have to justify or apologize. The wisdom she absorbed in life and probably here in this garden manifested itself in that sword and in that decisive moment.

"Actually, I don't think she had to give her actions much thought. Her instincts and cultural training took over, and, after killing the evil ones in the room, she gave the sword to you to set on her mantle. Do you realize what a magnificent gesture that was, to give control of everyone's life to you, the man who killed her husband?

"It happened just as instinctively as when she struck down the men who were going to kill her son, daughter- in-law and granddaughter.

Her inner peace has matured into a calm wisdom that transcends decision-making. When you have reached that level of wisdom, your response is automatic and potentially lethal or potentially life giving. We can be thankful that it was the latter when she looked at you.

"You will remember that there was no anger in her face when she dispatched the three, just a calm assurance of what needed to be done. Doing what is necessary to protect your family is never a tough decision to make. That is why the tyrants that take us to war always insist that we will be protecting our families and homeland. Only when they say it, it is mostly hogwash, an American expression I believe."

"Will they let her keep the sword?"

"It is a Japanese treasure, so I doubt that they will let it stay in her home more than a few weeks. Then the authorities will transfer it to the National Museum. They will provide twenty-four hour protection for it while it stays in Madam Maruyama's home to keep it out of the wrong hands. She will be paid handsomely for it, of course, and the family will be able to live their lives in comfort with the proceeds."

I was happy with the outcome.

The sun was now dropping low on the horizon and the long shadows were forming an added glow on the garden in front of us. The new shadows seem to cast a magic spell on the already tranquil scene and emphasized the sharp contrast of the large boulders protruding out of the pebbles against the white sand that had been raked into long ridges.

"Look Ray, at that rock over there shaped like a boat, sitting on sand that is formed as waves. It is said that the builders of this garden searched for years to find the exact boat-shaped rock. It symbolizes the journey that we all take on the ocean of life to reach the goal of infinite wisdom. In Buddhism 'infinite wisdom' is called Nirvana. "This entire garden is a metaphor symbolizing the life we live and the choices we make. No one can take the journey for us, nor is anyone responsible for the choices we make. We will face many storms and setbacks along the way before completing the journey. Each setback is experienced for a reason that we don't necessarily understand. As the Buddha said, 'We can't change the direction the wind is blowing, but we can change the way our sails are set.'

"We can only hope that we are prepared to weather the storms that will be faced along the way. If we have not prepared ourselves in this life, we must try again in the next one. But we must never give up, just as a ship must continue to plow through the rough seas to get to its destination, as that rock sitting over there tells us.

"Madam Maruyama faced her big storm when she made the decision whether to kill you or not. But when the time came, she was prepared, and instead of killing you, she gave you the sword to place on her mantle. Would you be able to do that, Ray?"

After a few minutes, Mr. Suzuki continued. "Tell me Ray. Do you ever think about the wives and children of the soldiers you killed?"

I came out of my trance and looked over at Mr. Suzuki. "No, actually I have not. It never occurred to me that I had a choice when I pulled the trigger. I know that sounds a little like, 'I was only following orders.' But as I remember back on it, my friend Phil was killed because he made the split second decision not to kill a woman who was charging directly at him. He would probably be alive today if he had not made what turned out to be that particular life or death decision."

Mr. Suzuki responded, "Phil apparently had a split second to decide if he was going to kill a young woman carrying a baby or allow her to kill him. We spend our entire lives learning and then have a fraction of a second to decide. It doesn't seem fair does it? But at least he will not be lying awake at night wondering if he had done the right thing."

"Yes, but is the right decision worth dying for?"

"I don't know Ray, but it is worth considering. What does this garden tell you? Does it give you any insight into your own wisdom? I can't speak for your reality or judge your actions, especially in wartime. You are the only one who can do that. I only encourage you to continue to search inside yourself for answers that are appropriate for you.

"There is nothing more I can contribute to your journey Ray. If I have helped, I am happy; I'm certainly happy that we found the Maruyamas. Also, I greatly admire you for wanting to return the priceless sword. Now I must leave and head back to Tokyo. It has been wonderful knowing you, and I hope that we meet again." Mr. Suzuki rose, shook my hand, bowed and walked down the path, as I watched him disappear through the garden.

As the sun dipped farther toward the horizon, I continued to absorb the beauty of the centuries old garden until I could see it no more. I was in good health and would probably live well into my eighties, in contrast to the dozens, maybe hundreds of twenty-year-old enemies I had killed during the war. How many wives and children wished they could kill me tonight? But today one could have and did not.

I had not intended for this trip be anything more than a visit to my old friend's gravesite in Burma and a side trip to return the colonel's samurai sword to his descendants in Japan. I certainly had not thought that this trip might be about learning a lesson or deciding whether or not I should have killed my enemies.

However, there was something about this place and the feeling I experienced while sitting there that felt familiar. Consequently, I could not dismiss it out of hand. Was I hearing my grandmother's teaching again, only in a different culture? Is it her voice that I heard as I sat there? No, it couldn't be. She lived and died ten thousand miles away from this garden. I've got to get home. This traveling is too much for me. I love it here in Japan, but I belong in New Mexico.

FIFTY-FOUR

I love my home state of New Mexico. My Native American grandmother had been a member of the Pueblo tribe, and she had passed on to me a special affection for their land and culture. On the flight home I relived the precious times I had spent with her listening to her stories and experiences in the American Southwest. My Mexican ancestors had migrated north sometime in the late seventeenth century and had built a home in the ancient city the Spanish called Santa Fe, Holy Faith.

I had been raised Catholic, but I had left my ancestral religion as a teenager. My mother half-jokingly reminded me that I would end up in hell if I didn't return to the Faith. I listened to her arguments with some amusement, hoping that she was wrong, because my experiences and my version of reality did not match hers.

I had continued to search for a faith that made more sense to me but hadn't been successful. When the war came, I hoped that new experiences would provide spiritual insights. I had heard that there were no atheists in foxholes, but I soon found that it was not true for me.

This day I felt I needed to get out, and, after driving a few miles west along my favorite dirt road, I stopped my car and wandered out onto the desert, walking toward the Rio Grande River. My wife and children had given me a warm welcome on my return from Burma and Japan, but my son, Mark, had been away at college. I was very happy to be home, but something was bothering me. I needed to walk out on the desert by myself.

I had stopped in San Francisco to tell Phil's wife, Janice, what had happened. She thanked me for returning the samurai sword to its owner, a sword that had been sitting on her mantle since 1945. She was stunned at my story but was happy that it had ended well for me. I hadn't told her that a Burmese woman fighting to free her homeland from foreigners had killed Phil. How would she react to the fact that her husband had died rather than kill a young mother and her baby whom he didn't even know. I had thought about this dilemma on the flight home and had decided not to mention it. Instead I told her a story of a noble death marked by the enemy's suicide charges, ending in heroic stands of a great leader and brave soldier. It struck me how similar the story of Phil's death that I told to Janice was to the one I had told to Madam Maruyama in Kyoto. Come to think about it, I wonder if Janice believed me any more than the colonel's wife had.

I had never before thought about the soldiers I had killed nor of their families. Killing was something I was trained to do and did very well. I had been able to convince myself that the men I killed were not really people, just the enemy. They certainly could have killed me, just as easily if I had not acted first. Had I been wrong all these years in thinking that killing an enemy was natural and normal and not to be questioned?

I stared down at the muddy Rio Grande flowing south and thought about the ancient Americans who had lived along this river for ten thousand years or more. Many of my ancestors were driven here from their four-corners home in the Southwest by a major drought that had struck the area in the fifteenth century. I wondered how that migration must have changed the lives of my ancestors who had survived the trek. I sat down on a large rock overlooking the river. Suppose that no one answered the call when our leaders declared war on another country. Suppose each one of us had said no to the recruiting officer who had tried to glorify the act of killing someone just to get us to sign-up. Suppose each of us had just turned around and went back home to tend our flocks and raise our families. Mark's words rang in my ears. Or was this my grandmother talking to me, or was it the rock garden in Kyoto? I was surprised by the similarity of their messages.

I thought about my grandparents' Taos neighbor, Kit Carson, the famous sidekick of John C. Fremont in the middle nineteenth century. As I was growing up, my granddad had told me about the great guide and scout. Kit had killed Indians in the West and Mexicans in California in the war of 1846. He was also a colonel in the Union Army during the Civil War.

My granddad had told me that when he was a boy Kit had shared with him that his biggest regret was killing three unarmed Mexican civilians in California's Marin County at the beginning of the war with Mexico. Jose Berreyessa and two friends were unarmed Mexican civilians who were visiting family in Marin County when they stumbled across a group of Fremont's angry California soldiers led by Carson. Kit pulled out his pistol and shot the three innocent men without justification or warning.

I wonder if Kit ever went to sleep at night without remembering that incident. In times of war against our fellow human beings we commit acts that we would never otherwise consider. War gives us excuses to do things that would shock and disgust us in normal times. We are sometimes turned into savages by war.

How do we return to being a caring and considerate part of a community when the war ends? Sometimes we can't. Sometimes we can only survive by living alone, by surviving in the wilderness. It is hard to face the reality of one's actions. My Spanish ancestors killed the Navajos living in New Mexico and Arizona. So does that make it even that Americans killed my Mexican relatives living in California?

All these thoughts were making me tired, so I put down my head and closed my eyes thinking about the fighting and killing I had seen in Burma.

As I sat on the rock nodding and looking across the desert, I thought I could hear the faint howl of a coyote calling for its mate. No, it's just the wind blowing up the canyon. I was startled when I heard it again; it seemed almost human.

I turned northeast looking toward the Sangre De Christo Mountains where my dad and I had hunted and fished when I was a teenager. I thought that if my dad's spirit were anywhere, it would be in those mountains.

Then I heard the sound again. This time it was all around me. Now I heard the rhythm of an Indian chant. As I tried to close my eyes, I suddenly saw the dancing of thousands of Native Americans who had lived in this valley throughout the centuries. Some were dressed in war bonnets, and some were women carrying their children on their backs like the Burmese women who tried to run us out of their country. Was that my grandmother leading the chant? What were the spirits trying to tell me?

Now the chants were louder, sounds swirling all around me. "The story is the same," I heard a dancing warrior say. "It is not Burmese, Japanese or American Indian, it is human. You cannot escape the consequences of your actions." I could swear that I heard my grandmother speaking to me directly and saying, "Yet, your life doesn't have to be ruled by them either."

The wind was now swirling around me as the dust blew up in clouds. I covered my head with my hands and tried to understand what the spirit was telling me. I thought about Phil and wished he were here. "I am right here my friend," I thought I heard. "But there is nothing more that I can do for you now that you aren't doing for yourself. You are asking the right questions and your life has given you insights that you would never have had otherwise. Come out to this rock soon and we will talk again," his voice trailed off in the wind.

"Wait Phil. I have so many questions to ask you." Was I talking to myself? I heard no answer, but I thought I could make out Phil's outline in the dust cloud in the distance. I was shocked to make out a woman standing next to Phil in Burmese dress smiling at me. My God, is that Nang, I thought.

The sun broke through, and the silhouettes disappeared. I could now make out the tops of the buildings in Taos to the north. No, it can't be, I thought; Taos is too far north. The air turned silent in the afternoon heat.

I sat for hours without moving. For some reason, and for the first time, I thought about the Japanese soldiers I had killed at Myitkyina and in the Burmese jungle. I thought about the Burmese women I had killed to protect our men on their way home, and, above all, I thought about the innocent civilians we had killed by blowing up a bridge because someone had told us that they were the enemy. As I thought about them, it came to me. War is indeed hell, and you carry that hell with you for the rest of your life. I hadn't believed in heaven or in a benevolent God since I'd left the Church. I had become convinced that it all ended with death. This became more evident to me as I witnessed the senseless killing of young men and women, some at my own hands, on both sides in the heat of war. Now I was not so sure about heaven. Just because I cannot see them, it doesn't mean that Ray, my dad and grandmother aren't there waiting for me. I guess I have more to learn before its time to go. I shook my head trying to clear the cobwebs.

I had experienced things in my life that most people only hear about. But I had a lot more to learn. How strange it was to me that the messages I had heard in Japan and Burma and learned from my paternal grandmother seemed to be the same. Now, it seemed to me, it was time to listen. I turned around on the rock and glanced toward the setting sun. The desert was indeed beautiful; but it was a different beauty that I had seen in the Kyoto gardens. Maybe there was a connection, I thought as I walked back toward my car.

Before I could get up, I felt the presence of my father around me. I remembered how he had taught me to track deer and listen for the coyote. I looked northeast toward the Sangre De Christos once again, but this time I saw a faint silhouette of two people walking away. I swore that I could see my father and Native American grandmother walking off toward the Sangre De Christos together, each carrying a hunting rifle.

As the two began to disappear into the haze of the mountains, I could have sworn that my dad turned back toward me and said, "Keep searching Ray. You are on the right track. Your grandmother and I will be waiting for you at our old hunting site when the time is right to go hunting together again." With tears in my eyes, I looked down at the desert sand in front of me, ground that my ancestors had walked on for so many years. I have spent my life searching, but maybe there are no answers, only questions.

My head jerked up and my eyes opened suddenly. I stared around and noticed that the sun was setting in the west. I reached up, rubbed my eyes and yawned. Had I been dreaming? I stood up and looked around while rubbing my sore back. I must have been dreaming, but it sure had seemed real, I thought, as I turned back toward my car. Anyway, it was time to go home and see my family. Maybe I would continue my search there.

FIFTY-FIVE

My life now pretty much revolves around my grandchildren. As I move into my eighties without my wife who died five years ago, there is nothing as important as those two kids. Actually I have four grandchildren, but the other two live with my daughter and her husband in Colorado. I see them a couple of times a year during the holidays, but I see Carol and Butch, my son's children, every day.

My son and my daughter-in-law, Becky, insisted that I move in with them when my back finally went out permanently, and I had to use a wheelchair to move around. Mark and Becky built a grandfather room on the back of their house. I have my own bathroom and personal reading area. My son Mark is now the president of the construction firm that I started when I got back from the war, and it is doing extremely well. I am happy that we moved up to Taos. I love being closer to the Sangre de Christo Mountains, and I sit out here on the patio and just stare at them.

I don't get down to my favorite spot near the Rio Grande River any more; driving anywhere has become impossible. I often think about that spot and the many times I tried to recreate my one experience there with my friend Phil, my dad and my grandmother. I still can't figure out if it was a dream or something real. I guess it doesn't matter. It was real to me.

My granddaughter, Carol, climbed up on my lap a few weeks ago and said, "Grandpa. Would you please write about your experiences of the war so we can know what you went through?" How could I refuse? So here it is. But then Becky, my daughter-in-law sitting nearby asked for another favor. "Dad, could you write us a story on how we should live our lives, something we could read when you are no longer here. You have given us so many good things to think about, but nobody thought to write them down. Mark, the kids and I really hope that you will do this for us."

Well, writing about my war experiences is one thing. Telling my kids and grandchildren how to live their lives is quite another. Putting on paper my "rules for living" is not easy and requires some real thought. However, I love my granddaughter because she is so cute, and she joined her mother and insisted. I guess I'll give it a try.

<u>To My Grandchildren</u>

- Nothing lasts forever, not you, not me, not life.
- Be happy and satisfied with what you have because you are not going to get any more, and you will waste your time trying.
- Get up off the mat and put up your dukes. Next time you will know enough to dodge his swing.
- There is no particular reason why you lost.
- The world is not particularly so that wishing were will not make it so.
- Hope is not a plan.
- Being good and honest often does not pay off, and there is no compensation for misfortune.
- You have the responsibility to be good and honest anyway.
- Don't ever fail to help someone in need whether he deserves it or not.
- When you ride on the back of a tiger, be careful when you get off.
- You can't make anyone love you, so don't even try.
- Don't blame God for losing. God doesn't care if you win or lose.

- Keeping our world safe and under control is critical. Remember, it's the only one we have and we are all in it together.
- Treat evil with pity. If you look hard enough, maybe you can understand it.
- Love may not be enough, but sometimes it's all we have.
- Never assume a damn thing.
- We are born alone, and we die alone. We must accept that we are all ultimately alone.
- The most important responsibility we have in life is to learn about ourselves. No one can do that for us.
- We must keep struggling toward solutions. Nothing worthwhile comes on the first try.
- Life is filled with ambiguities. We must learn to live with them.
- Tomorrow is a new day. Forget how you screwed up today and get on with tomorrow.
- We have partial freedom, partial power and partial knowledge. So what!
- All of life's important decisions must be made with insufficient data.
- We are responsible for all we do. There is no devil that made us do it.
- No excuses will be accepted, so don't try.
- "I was ordered to do it by my superior," is not an acceptable excuse. You are the one that makes the final decision.
- You are free to do whatever you like. You must be prepared to live with the consequences.
- Only you can forgive yourself. No one else matters.
- Gambling is the worst. When you lose, you think that it was bad luck. When you win, you think you deserved it. Neither is true.
- Nothing can make up for the absence of someone we love, but we must go on in spite of the loss.
- The important things in life are simple. If you try to make a religion out of them, they will elude you.

- Take care of both those who are deserving and those who are not.
- Music is the road to inner peace. Select yours carefully.
- Abandon any mental bias born of religion or culture.
- Stop striving after admiration. It will come when you least expect it.
- Sometimes bad people win. Live with it.
- When your mind is preoccupied with the ideas of the past and the images of the future, it overlooks the joy of the moment.
- All misery is created by the activity of the mind.
- Can you be still and look inside?
- Your character is determined by the energies to which you devote yourself.
- Who can gather material things and ignore the suffering in the world?
- Knowing that daybreak will come, we can all sleep peacefully at night.
- The important things in life come from listening, thinking, reading and meditating.
- Arrogance and anger are the greatest hindrance to being happy.
- Let go of your obsessions.
- Take nothing into your body that will cause addiction. The simplest things taken too often can kill.

So there you are my grandchildren, words to live by that I have developed over the years. Keep them handy and give them to your grandchildren along with some of your own. My life will be over soon and I will join your grandmother in what lies beyond. Have I learned enough? Not by half. But I will keep searching and may have more to share with you when we meet again. I love you.

ADDENDUM

This story is based upon a combination of battles and people that are both real and imagined. The epic battle of Myitkyina, Burma, near the China and India borders was real, and it did occur in the summer of 1944 as described here. It is a strategic town in Northern Burma and is adjacent to the Irawwaddi River. It was an important link on the Ledo Road, America's main supply route to China after the Burma Road was captured by the Japanese early in the war. The battle is described in Wikipedia.

The story of Merrill's Marauders is generally true as is the escape of Japanese forces under Colonel Maruyama, both recorded in Wikipedia. He escaped from Myitkyina into the Burmese jungle, and then seems to have disappeared from the history books. This story is a fictitious account of what might have happened to him.

The exploits of Sergeant Hashimoto in Burma are recorded in the history books, although no name is given for this courageous Nisei. For this novel, he was given a fictitious name.

Some of the battles that Major Jenkins and his men were involved in did happen in various parts of the China theatre. Friends who actually participated in them related them to the author. None have been recorded as far as the author knows.

Basically, all the officers above the rank of major, except Colonel Stevenson, actually existed in the war and can be found various history books and in Wikipedia. Everyone below the rank of colonel is fictional as is the story of the troop's exploits in Burma and Captain Beltrans' adventures in Japan.

The legendary Japanese sword maker, Miyairi Akihira, did exist and is unquestionably the master sword maker in modern Japan. He died in the post-war era. The famous Honjo Masamune Sword, a national Japanese treasure as found in Wikipedia did/does exist. It disappeared at the end of World War II and has not been returned to Japan as of this writing. Perhaps someone reading this story will recognize its importance to the Japanese culture and will return it to its rightful owners. The beautiful Zen Garden described in this story is in Kyoto and is only one of several. It is impossible to describe all of them adequately in words. They are all worth a visit by anyone interested in their exceptional beauty and in the Zen and Samurai traditions of Japan.

The author has visited them all and describes the one in this story as he remembers it.

Of course, the tales of Kit Carson appear in his biography and books of the Mexican American War as told here. However, nothing has been written as far as the author knows regarding how he felt about killing Jose Berreyessa and his two unarmed friends in Marin County during America's war with Mexico in the 1840's. His boss, John C. Fremont is reported in history books to have told him that, "We have no room for prisoners." Even Americans living at the time apparently believed that this was no excuse for killing three innocent and unarmed men. Maybe this event contributed to Fremont's defeat as the Republican candidate for president in 1856.

Any similarity to this story and actual events and people, other than those outlined here, is purely coincidental. All of the characters and events in Japan other than the famous sword maker, Miyairi Akihira, are fictional.

ACKNOWLEDGEMENTS

I am deeply indebted to the members of my family who encouraged me to write this story. My late daughter, Diana Marie Edwards had been after me for years to write a book and her life has been an inspiration to me. It is a supreme tragedy that she has not lived to see the results of her encouragement. She is buried in her hometown of Palo Alto and I dedicate this, my first book, to her memory.

Without the review, suggestions and corrections made by my wife, Shirley, this book would not have been possible. I also owe a debt of gratitude to the many friends who have read it and offered suggestions as I went along, including, but not limited to my wonderful editor, Jennifer LaForce also friends Susan Hunn and Charlotte Higgins.

I offer a special thanks to my twelfth grade English teacher, Mrs. Busby, who gave me the worst grade I received in high school. But she saw promise in me and tried to convince me that even engineers should become proficient in English. I wish I had paid more attention to her. I have lost track of her since graduation and presume that, since she was ten years older than I, she is probably not alive today. If she is and reads this, I hope she is proud of her wayward student and remembers that some things take longer in life to learn than others.

I offer a deep debt of gratitude to my old friend from Lockheed days, Joe Tueller, who has written a number of great fiction books since retiring. His inspiration has confirmed that even engineers can write stories, validating what Mrs. Busby tried to teach me in 1950.